A Thuggish, Ruggish Love 2
Heart of a Gangsta

By

Regina Swanson

Remember….
You haven't read 'til you've read #Royalty
Check us out at www.royaltypublishinghouse.com
#royaltydropsdopebooks

Text ROYALTY to 42828 for sneak peeks and
notifications when they come out!

Looking for a publishing home?

Royalty Publishing House, Where the Royals reside, is accepting submissions for writers in the urban fiction genre. If you're interested, submit the first 3-4 chapters with your synopsis to submissions@royaltypublishinghouse.com. Check out our website for more information: www.royaltypublishinghouse.com.

Be sure to <u>LIKE</u> our Royalty Publishing House page on Facebook

CHAPTER ONE
KEYA

"Mrs. Thomas, we need to speak with you about what happened to your husband," the police detective stated.

"Yes," Keya budded in before Aleah could respond. "What happened to your husband?"

"Keya, please calm down," Aleah said.

"Don't tell me to fucking calm down when my brother is in there fighting for his life," Keya screamed.

"Mrs. Thomas, we really need you to tell us more about the man that shot your husband," the detective insisted.

Aleah hated that he said that in front of Keya.

"What man?" Keya bellowed.

"Detective, can we talk somewhere else?" Aleah asked. She knew she wouldn't be able to concentrate on the lie that she was about to tell, if Keya was budding in every second.

"Hell naw, you can talk to him right here, right now," Keya barked.

"Ma'am, you are really going to have to calm down and let us do our jobs," the detective spoke to Keya. "Once we have all the details, I promise that we will give you a full update."

"What the fuck ever," Keya responded.

"Are you prepared to go down to the station to give a statement?" he asked Aleah.

"Yes," she told him.

"Really, Aleah? Your husband is in emergency surgery and you're going to leave the hospital without knowing if he lives or dies?" Keya was relentless. Her emotions were on one-hundred.

Aleah sighed. "I'll be right back Keya."

"Don't even bother. I'll see to my brother because you damn sure aren't."

Aleah was hating this. She wanted to be there for Keya, but she was making it difficult. Aleah thought about how she was going to respond when she found out the whole fake truth.

"Can we do this somewhere in the hospital?" Aleah decided.

The detective turned to the hospital staff, asking if they had a private room that they could use. The head nurse directed them to one of the doctor's offices. Keya tried to follow them inside of the room, but the detective stopped her.

"Miss, I need you to wait out here."

Thank God, Aleah thought.

The officer closed the door in Keya's face. She was pissed, but there was nothing that she could do about it.

Keya decided to stay close by the door. She wanted to try to listen in if she could, on anything that Aleah had to say.

"Would you like anything to drink?" the officer asked.

"Yes, thank you," Aleah replied. "A cup of water would be great."

The detective walked over to the water dispenser, filled a cup and handed it to Aleah. Then he took out a mini-recorder. "Do you mind if I record our conversation?"

Aleah paused. She wasn't sure if it was a good idea or not. If she said yes, she might say something wrong and he would have it on tape. But if she said she didn't want to be recorded, he might think that she had something to hide.

"No, I don't mind," she decided.

"Great, can you tell me whose home you were in tonight?" he asked.

"Blaze Carter," she answered.

Keya had her ear glued to the door. *Did she just say Blaze Carter?*

"What were you doing at Mr. Carter's home?" he continued.

"I was invited over for dinner," she answered.

"You and your husband had been invited to Mr. Carter's home for dinner?"

"No. Well, yes. It's complicated." Aleah was getting nervous. She'd forgotten that she wasn't supposed to mention Mackie, so she couldn't say that Xavier had come to meet Mackie.

"Which is it Mrs. Thomas?" he questioned.

"I was invited to dinner. My husband wasn't. He must have tracked me to Blaze's house," Aleah answered.

"You said tracked you, were you having an affair with Mr. Carter?"

Keya was in shock. She was pissed and confused. *How does Aleah even know Blaze Carter*, she thought.

"I don't know," Aleah answered.

"You don't know if you were having an affair or not?" the detective asked.

Aleah struggled to get her words out. "If you are asking if I was sleeping with Blaze Carter, the answer is no. But we have been spending time together just getting to know each other."

Keya couldn't believe it. She tried to think back. *When did Aleah have time to spend with Blaze? And when did she start seeing him?* She couldn't think of anything unusual that Aleah had been doing.

"Did your husband know about any of this?" he questioned.

"I didn't think so," Aleah told him. "But he showed up at Blaze's house."

"And what happened?" the detective questioned.

"Xavier pushed me up against the wall when he saw me. He yelled 'Are you fucking that nigga?' He had his hands around my neck. He was squeezing so hard.

I tried my best to scratch at Xavier's hands. He was cutting off my air supply, making it hard for me to breathe. He pinned me against the wall to keep me from moving. He had his knee jammed into my private area. I was in so much pain. I tried to call Blaze. He was in the kitchen finishing up the dinner when I went to answer the door, but it was like Xavier had a vise grip on my windpipe and I couldn't say more than a whisper.

Then Xavier yelled, Oh, you calling for that nigga to come save you. I will fuck both of all asses up.'

Blaze must have heard the bumping because he came in and saw me pinned against the wall. Blaze was confused, he asked Xavier what he was doing. Blaze told him to take his hands off of me.

'This is my goddamned wife,' Xavier told him.

'I don't give a shit,' Blaze said, as he used his elbow to jab a sharp blow to Xavier's back.

The pain Blaze sent through Xavier's body caused him to release me. I fell to the floor, coughing and gasping for air. Xavier was staggering.

Blaze bent down to me asking me if I was ok.

I nodded my head yes.

I guess that must have pissed Xavier off even more, seeing Blaze bending down tending to me. That's when Xavier picked up the vase that was sitting on top of the piano. He used it to slam it down across Blaze's head. Blaze fell to the floor. They fought.

The next thing I remember is that I heard a gunshot, and Xavier fell to the ground."

"Whose gun was it?" the detective asked.

"I don't know; I didn't see who pulled it out. Everything was happening so face," Aleah explained.

Keya had heard enough. She burst into the room. "You know good and goddamn well Xavier does not own a fucking gun. Blaze Carter's thuggish ass shot my brother because you were having an affair, and now you are trying to cover for that motherfucker."

Keya turned to the detective. "Do you know that he is a damn drug dealer? Yeah Aleah, you left that bit of information out. Your boyfriend and his bitch ass sister sell drugs for a living."

Keya could tell that Aleah was surprised. "Oh, he didn't tell you that, huh? I guess that's on a need-to-know basis."

Aleah was sick of the attitude that she was getting from Keya. "You know what Keya… you know better than anybody the hell that your brother has put me through. He would have killed me tonight if Blaze hadn't…" Aleah stopped. She couldn't finish her words.

"Hadn't what, shot my brother in the back?" Keya yelled. She charged at Aleah, tackling her. They both hit the floor with a big thump.

It was a full on chick fight. Aleah was tired of being other people's punching bag. She fought Keya back. Keya was tough but Aleah was pissed. Both were swinging and flailing their arms as hard and as fast as they could. Keya was trying to get revenge for Xavier, and Aleah was trying to let out all of her hurt emotions that she was feeling since she married Xavier.

"Stop that," the detective yelled. It was a weak response from him. He didn't give a shit if they got their frustrations out, but he had to sound as though he were concerned. He was secretly hoping one of them got their shirt ripped off and a breast popped out. He used this time as an opportunity to get the cup that Aleah had held. He placed it in a Ziploc baggie. He wanted to have it tested.

One minute, Keya was on top looking like she had the upper hand. Then Aleah would flip her and commence to trying to whip Keya's ass.

"Ladies," the detective tried to sound interested.

When a few nurses ran into the room, the detective moved in to try to stop the fight. He was smiling, having gotten his wish. Aleah's shirt was torn and he had a close up view of her bright red bra with half her breasts sticking out. The only thing that he couldn't see was her nipple. Both Aleah and Keya's hair were all over their heads.

"If Xavier dies, it's all your fucking fault," Keya huffed.

CHAPTER TWO
Mackie

Mackie felt like she was dying inside. She had finally found someone that she thought was connecting with. Her tears wouldn't stop. She couldn't remember how she had managed to get to the Preston Wood's location, but here she was pulling into the driveway. She saw Diesel's car already parked. When he saw Mackie pull up, he came out of the house to meet her at the car.

Mackie sat motionless in the driver's seat. He opened the door, reached in, and pulled Mackie out of the car. No words needed to be spoken. He saw the pain etched across her face. Diesel picked her up and carried her back into the house. She buried her head in his chest and cried her eyes out.

Diesel didn't ask questions and he didn't need to know details. He hated seeing her this way. She was the strongest person that he knew. To see her at such a weak moment tugged at his heart. Mackie felt like Diesel was a part of her family. He was more than just her right hand. They were connected. When one of them hurt, they both hurt.

Mackie tried to talk to Diesel once they were inside. Diesel couldn't understand a thing she was saying. Her words were jumbled and she sounded like a two-year-old babbling. Diesel shushed her and rubbed her back.

"Whatever it is, I'll fix it," he told her.

Mackie shook her head. She knew this was something that no one could fix. She'd killed the love of her life. Mackie cried harder just thinking about it.

"I'm bad. I'm evil," she cried.

Diesel was finally able to understand her.

"You're not evil," he consoled.

"I kill people," Mackie stated.

Diesel didn't know what to say. She did kill people, they all did. It was a part of the game.

Mackie's chest continued to heave up and down.

"We only kill bad people." It was the only thing he could think of to say.

Mackie shook her head no. "I kill innocent people too."

Diesel was at a disadvantage. He didn't know where all of this was coming from. He couldn't help Mackie if he didn't know what had happened. Blaze had only said get to Preston Wood, Mackie needs you.

Diesel told his girl, Shay, that he had to go because Mackie needed him. She was pissed. They were supposed to be spending a quiet night together. They sent their son to her mother's house so that they could have some alone time. Shay was sick of Mackie always calling on Diesel at all times of the night, and Diesel dropping everything and running to be by her side like a little lap dog.

Shay knew the type of work Diesel did. It was one of the reasons that she'd initially tried to get with him. She wanted to be taken care of and live the lifestyle of the rich and thuggish. And everybody associated with the Carter's had money flowing from their pockets like a waterfall. Shay had her eye on Blaze at first. She had been trying her best to get next to him, but Mackie was always cock blocking, at least that's what she would tell her friends. When she got tired of trying to get around Mackie, she decided to go after Diesel.

Diesel turned out to be the perfect man for her. He acted like he really liked her and would do anything for her and their son, unless Mackie needed something. Shay thought that things would change and he would start to put her first once she'd gotten pregnant. That thought was quickly shot down on the day she went into labor, and Diesel told her he couldn't make it to the hospital because he was handling something for Mackie. It was on that day that Shay truly started to hate Mackie.

Diesel knew that Shay would be pissed off for about a week after he left her alone tonight. He did care about Shay. She was the mother of his son, but Mackie was number one in his heart. She always had been and always would be. Mackie was his boss and friend. But if he thought for a second that she would consider him to be more than that, he would drop Shay with the quickness. But Diesel knew that he wasn't the type of brother that Mackie wanted, so he played his position and catered to her every chance that he got. He settled for being her right hand.

Mackie was still sitting on his lap with her head nestled in his chest. Her whimpers were starting to fade. Diesel figured that she was starting to doze off to sleep. He continued to rub her back in soothing motions. He kissed her on her head. The love that he felt for her would never go away. When he heard her lightly snoring, he stood up carrying her to the bedroom. He gently laid her in the bed and removed her shoes. He pulled the covers up over her body, tucking her in.

Before Diesel could leave the room, his phone rang waking up Mackie. She looked up at him and slightly smiled. Diesel smiled back as he answered the phone.

"What's up Shay?

Mackie listened to the one-sided conversation. She disliked Shay just as much as Shay disliked her. She kept that bit of information to herself. She didn't want to speak negatively about Diesel's girl. But she knew that Shay was just a gold digger, trying to get as much as she could from anybody willing to be her sponsor.

She remembered Shay trying to get with Blaze, but she wasn't having it.

"I'm not sure," Diesel said.

Mackie figured Shay must have been asking him what time he was coming home. Diesel kept his eyes on Mackie the entire time that he was talking to Shay. Mackie was getting irritated. She didn't feel like Diesel needed to explain his every move to Shay. She understood that they had a son together, but she knew that Shay used their son like a pawn in her silly game to hold on to Diesel.

Mackie pushed the covers back and stood up. She reached for the tail of her shirt and pulled it over her head. Diesel tried not to stare but couldn't keep his eyes off of her breasts. It was a beautiful sight to see. Mackie wore a teal colored lace bra. When she pulled her jeans down and stepped out of them, Diesel saw that she wore the same color matching panties. Mackie had no clue what the sight of her in nothing but a bra and panties, was doing to Diesel. Her mind was still on Xavier.

"Damn," Diesel said when she turned to walk into the restroom. Mackie thought he was talking to Shay. Shay was asking him, "Damn what?" Only Diesel knew he was responding to the sight of Mackie's plump ass as she left the room. "I'll call you back Shay." Diesel hung up before Shay had a chance to respond.

Diesel knew he needed to get control of his testosterone. The sight of Mackie's almost naked body had awakened his sleeping giant. Diesel sat down in the chair removing his shoes. He closed his eyes and starting doing some breathing exercises that he had seen people use on TV to calm themselves down.

"Breath in, hold, hold, hold, release." Diesel kept repeating the words in his head. Mackie walked back out of the bathroom with an oversized t-shirt on. She looked at Diesel for a moment as he breathed in and out.

"What are you doing?" she asked.

Diesel opened one eye to peek at her. "Thank God," he mumbled. He was glad that she was now covered.

"Nothing, just a few relaxation techniques that I learned," he replied.

"Shay bugging again, huh," Mackie guessed.

"Yeah," Diesel lied.

"You can go if you want. I'll be alright," Mackie told him.

She really didn't want him to go, but she knew she had no right to try to keep him from his so called family. Mackie sat down on the bed and waited for his response.

"I'm cool," Diesel told her. "Shay understands."

Mackie looked at him sideways.

"Ok, maybe she doesn't. But she knows that I have things to do."

Mackie smiled. She was glad that Diesel was there with her. She scooted over to the middle of the bed and told Diesel, "Come lay with me."

Diesel didn't move. He wanted to stay glued to the chair that he was sitting in.

"D," Mackie said again.

"Huh?" He pretended that he hadn't heard her request.

"Come lay with me," she said again. "I won't bite. You're like a brother to me."

Diesel reluctantly got up and slowly walked over to the bed. He stiffly laid down in the bed, being careful not to touch Mackie.

Mackie turned her back to him. She slid back and reached across her body, grabbing his arm, pulling him on his side. She wrapped his arm around her waist. She'd put them in a position to spoon.

Diesel cursed his body for betraying him once again. He started his breathing exercises again. "Breath in, hold, hold, hold, release." It wasn't working.

Mackie's eyes popped open when she felt Diesel's big hard dick poking her in the ass. She laughed. "Diesel you better put that damn thing away." Mackie assumed he was thinking about his girl. "I'm not Shay."

CHAPTER THREE
BLAZE

On the ride to the police station, Blaze continued to go over the story in his mind. He wanted it to flow when they started asking him questions about what had happened. Blaze was finding it hard to concentrate. His mind was on Mackie and how she was holding up. He hoped that Diesel was with her keeping her calm. Mackie did everything hard, including taking on guilt that wasn't hers alone. He knew that shooting Xavier was going to have her messed up for a while. He could tell that she really cared for him. Blaze still couldn't get over the fact that Aleah's husband is the same Xavier that's been dating Mackie.

Blaze had initially thought that Xavier was good for Mackie. But knowing what Aleah had told him about her abusive husband, there was no way in hell he was going to let Mackie date him, even if he survived. Blaze couldn't stand weak ass men that hit and disrespected women. He would protect Mackie and Aleah both before he let Xavier lay another hand on either of them.

When they arrived at the station, the officers pulled the police car up to the Sally Port to walk him through booking. All of this was new to him. He and Mackie had never been arrested before. As a matter of fact, they'd never even received a ticket. They both knew how to fly under the radar. Not to mention, any number of their people would be willing to trade places with them by taking the wrap for whatever was needed.

Blaze walked over to the desk where he was fingerprinted, photographed and given a tan jumpsuit to put on, before being placed into a holding cell. Blaze knew one of the guys in the holding cell. He worked over on the west side overseeing everything from the trinity to uptown.

"What the fuck are you doing in here man?" Blaze asked. Blaze was strict about his people not being arrested and drawing attention to the organization. He didn't have time for fuck ups.

"Nothing to do with the business," he told Blaze.

Blaze stared at him waiting for him to elaborate.

"My girl called the police on me… said I hit her," he said.

Blaze had zero tolerance for foolishness. He made a mental note to ex this fool. He didn't care if his girl was lying or not. It was petty shit that put people on the police's radar. Blaze walked over and sat down on the bench. As soon as he sat down, his name was called.

"Blaze Carter," the detention officer yelled, "Cuff up."

Blaze stood up, walked to the door and turned around, so the officer could place the handcuffs on his wrists. He figured it was time to tell the detectives what happened. He wished they were calling him because he had made bail. But he hadn't had a bail hearing yet. Khalil should have contacted his lawyer by now. Blaze wasn't trying to give any statements without his lawyer being present.

He walked Blaze to the last room on a long hallway. When Blaze walked into the room, he was shocked. It wasn't a detective with the police department. Two agents dressed in jeans, t-shirts, and black jackets with the letters DEA written across it, were waiting for him.

Blaze cursed in his mind, *Fuck*. He knew once you were on the DEA or FBI's radar, it was a total different ball game. By the time they decided to come after you, nine times out of ten, they already had enough evidence to convict your ass. Blaze hoped he was that tenth person in the 9 times out 10 pool.

The officer removed the cuffs and closed the door, leaving Blaze alone with the agents. Blaze stood close to the door. He knew this could go either way for him. He needed to be smart.

"Mr. Carter, come on over, take a seat," one of the agents said.

Blaze did as instructed. He already knew he wasn't going to answer any questions without having his lawyer present, but he wanted to know what they knew.

"Mr. Carter, we aren't going to bullshit you. We want to get right to the point," the other agent said. "My name is Agent Blanton and this is partner Agent Zamora. I want us to be honest with each other. Can we agree to do that?"

Blaze thought, *here we go with the bullshit.*

"What happened at your house tonight is the least of your problems," Agent Blanton stated. "Xavier Thomas is expendable. Do you know what expendable means?"

Blaze just looked at him. Most people thought that drug dealers were dumb, but that was hardly the case with Blaze and Mackie. They both had done well in school, graduating at the top of their classes. Either of them could have gone on to medical school, law school or any other tech program of their choosing. But that wasn't the hand that they were dealt. They inherited an empire; a drug empire that had them at the top of the game.

"Expendable means something that's not worth keeping or maintaining," Agent Zamora budded in.

Blaze felt like he was dealing with Frick and Frack. He was sure that he outscored both of them on the SAT that his school counselor had convinced him to take his junior year in high school. Blaze damn near earned a perfect score on the test.

"But we aren't above using what we know about your attempted murder of Mr. Thomas to get what we want," Agent Blanton stated.

"What happened tonight was self-defense," Blaze uttered.

"That may be true Mr. Carter, but as I indicated before, you help us, and we'll help you," Agent Zamora added.

"And what is that you need help with?" Blaze questioned.

"We know all about the Carter Empire," they said in unison.

There it was, the words that Blaze had been dreading to hear. The Carter family was on the government's radar. Blaze cursed again in his head, *Fuck!* He had taken every possible precaution that he could to shield he and Mackie from the Feds. Blaze knew that once you were under their microscope, it was only a matter of time before they slammed the door shut on you.

Fuck, fuck, fuck, Blaze said over and over in his head, although he kept his poker face in place.

"Look gentlemen, I think you might have the wrong Carter," Blaze stated.

The agents perked up. "Exactly," Agent Zamora stated.

"You see Mr. Carter, we know that you are second in charge and a bit mild mannered. We want the leader of the Carter Clan. By the way, where is your sister?"

Blaze wanted to reach across the table and snap the agents' necks. He could do it before either of them knew what was happening. He would die before he let anything happen to Mackie. He needed to play it cool and not let them know that Mackie was his weakness. Once people knew your weakness, they went for it to fuck you up mentally.

"What's Mackie got to do with anything that you've said?" Blaze asked. He didn't give a shit what they were saying from this point on. He just needed to appease them until he could get out of there.

"I thought we agreed not to bullshit each other," Agent Blanton stated.

Blaze took his hands and slid them underneath his thighs. They truly didn't know how lethal he could be. He sat on his hands, to keep his reflexes in check when they said stupid shit.

"We know that Mackie is the brains behind your operation, and we want her off the streets. From what we can tell, she's a ruthless hothead that spreads fear throughout the entire community. We heard that you are the more sensible, calm one of the two." They swapped back and forth between each other, filling Blaze in on what they knew about him, Mackie and their family business.

"You basically have two choices Blaze," Agent Zamora said. Blaze recognized that she had called him Blaze that time. Agent Blanton looked at his partner crazily when she did it.

Blaze studied their body language. He could tell Blanton was the hard ass. His partner had a softer edge. Blaze looked at Agent Zamora; she was pretty decent looking. She probably would look even better, when she let her hair down out of that librarian style bun that she was sporting, throw away the black jeans and steel toe boots, and put a sexy little dress on her.

Blaze thought about what they had said earlier. He wasn't above using what he had to get what he wanted either. Blaze decided to test the waters. He looked at Agent Zamora and slid his tongue across his lips slowly, while giving her his undivided attention. She slightly shifted in her seat. *Bingo*, Blaze said in his head.

"So what's it going to be?" Agent Blanton asked. "Are you going to cooperate and help us get Mackie off the streets, or are we going to charge you with the attempted murder of Xavier Thomas?"

Before Blaze had a chance to speak, the door opened.

"Gentlemen, how many of my client's rights have you violated?" Blaze's attorney walked in barking at the agents for not following proper procedures. "You know as well as I do, anything that my client might have said to you will be inadmissible in court. Now if you don't mind, I'd like to speak to my client alone."

CHAPTER FOUR
ALEAH

The nurses had managed to separate Aleah and Keya. Aleah couldn't believe that Keya was acting the way she was. Aleah knew that people responded to stress in different ways, but for her to come after her physically was unforgivable. Aleah had spent much of her adult life being a victim of domestic abuse. She'd be damned if she let Xavier's little sister abuse her too. It was way past time for her to stand up for herself.

It's amazing the strength that you can gain from simply having someone in your corner. Blaze did that for her. He had given her, her self-dignity back. It was something that you couldn't put a price tag on, but she would definitely help him protect his little sister even though she was the woman that Xavier was sleeping with. Aleah knew that if Mackie had not shot Xavier, she and Blaze would both be dead right now. Xavier was just that pissed.

Aleah sat thinking, *men can run around and screw everything that moves, but the second that they find out that their wife or girlfriend has an interest in somebody else, they lose their damn minds.*

Aleah and Keya both sat in the waiting room. It was the last place that Aleah wanted to be, but she had to keep up appearances for the detective's sake. She really wanted to go check on Blaze. She was worried about him. She prayed that they didn't charge him with attempted murder. *If we just stick with our stories, it will be fine*, she told herself. *It was self-defense, which was partially true. Xavier had been the aggressor. We were only defending ourselves.* Aleah allowed her mind to wander to Mackie. She wondered how she was doing. She had seemed really distraught when she saw that she had shot Xavier.

How long had they been seeing each other? Aleah wondered. *How many times had they met at the condo? Was he planning on leaving me?* All of these were questions that only Xavier and Mackie could answer. She wouldn't be getting this knowledge anytime soon.

Keya continued to occasionally glance in Aleah's direction. She had so many questions that she wanted to ask Aleah, but she was too pissed right now to try to approach her. If she did, they would be rolling around on the floor again, trying to beat each other's brains out. Keya knew that Xavier had been an asshole to Aleah, but it didn't constitute to him losing his life.

Keya had started to calm down a little bit. Xavier was still in surgery, but her thinking was that the longer that he was in surgery, the better. That meant that the doctors were still working on him. The alternative was them coming out saying he didn't pull through, or saying that there was nothing else that they could do but wait.

Keya felt like she needed to apologize to Aleah. It was the right thing to do. She was in the middle of talking herself into going to sit next to Aleah and apologizing, when Aleah's phone rang.

The ringing of her phone pissed Keya off. Aleah's phone hardly ever rang. And when it did, it was always her or Xavier checking in with her. *Since I am not calling her and Xavier is laid up in surgery, that means that it has to be Blaze Carter calling,* Keya thought. Any thought of apologizing to Aleah went right out of Keya's head.

"I know damn well you don't have your fucking boyfriend calling while my brother is laid up in that damn hospital bed," Keya spewed.

Aleah sighed. "Chill Keya." When she looked at the phone, it was from a number that she didn't recognize, so it very well could have been Blaze calling.

"You fucking chill," Keya answered.

"I don't need this shit," Aleah said. She stood up walking towards the exit. When she got closer to the door, Keya snatched the phone from Aleah's hands. Without looking at the phone, Keya slammed the phone to the ground causing it to shatter into small pieces.

"You are so fucking childish and immature," Aleah screamed. She'd had enough of Keya's tantrum. "I'm out."

"Good! Bye, we don't need you," Keya yelled to her back as she walked from the room.

Aleah walked back to the emergency room exit. She didn't know what she was going to do. She had ridden to the hospital in the ambulance so she didn't have her car. In the midst of everything that was going on earlier, she had forgotten her purse at Blaze's house.

She paced back and forth. A small cold front was starting to blow in. She stuffed her hands in her pockets to warm them. When she did, she felt a card in her pocket. She smiled, remembering Blaze had given her the card, telling her that if she needed anything to call the number and ask for Khalil. *Blaze is still taking care of me even when he is not here. That's the type of love that I need*, Aleah thought.

Aleah walked back in the door and over to the nurse's station. She asked if she could use their phone. They directed her to a wall phone in the emergency room waiting area. She dialed the number and waited for someone to answer.

"May I speak to Khalil?"

"This is Khalil."

"Hi, my name is Aleah. Blaze gave me your number and told me to call you if I needed anything."

Aleah explained where she was and what she needed. Khalil said that he was on his way. She told him what she was wearing and that she would be standing outside of the emergency room.

"I'll be there in about fifteen minutes," he responded.

"Thanks," Aleah said.

She sat down in the chair next to the phone and placed her head in her hands. She wanted to scream, but that wouldn't help her or her situation. Aleah stood up and walked outside. She hoped that Khalil would pull up before Keya had a chance to come looking for her. She didn't want to have any more public altercations.

At exactly fifteen minutes from the time she had hung up the phone with Khalil, he pulled up, stopped in front of her and asked if she was Aleah.

"Yes," she answered. "I'm guessing you are Khalil."

"I am." He got out of the car and walked Aleah to the other side, opening the door for her. Aleah slid into the car and waited. Khalil closed the door and walked back to the driver's side. He got in and drove away. All the while, Aleah never knew that Keya had been watching her out of the window in the emergency room waiting area.

"Thank you for coming to pick me up," Aleah commented.

"You're welcome."

"I left my purse at Blaze's house. Do you mind taking me to pick it up?"

Khalil reached in the backseat and pulled her purse to the front.

"Thank you," Aleah dragged the word out.

"No problem," Khalil responded. "It's my job."

"If you could just drop me at my house, I can pick my car up," Aleah requested.

"Blaze asked me to bring you straight to the jail to visit with him."

"Oh," Aleah responded. She felt good and bad about that. It was good that he wanted to see her, but bad that it sounded like he was taking control of her. Aleah shook that feeling off. It was the result of low self-esteem. She could take anything that anybody said to her and find the negative in it. While most people only looked at or thought of the positive, she was the opposite.

CHAPTER FIVE
XAVIER

Although Xavier had laid on the floor bleeding unconscious from the bullet that Mackie had sent tearing through his flesh, he could hear everything that was going on around him. He heard how upset Mackie was when she realized that it was him that she'd shot. He wanted to hold her and tell her that he was okay, but he couldn't move. It was like he was having an out of body experience. He also heard Blaze telling her to leave and that he would handle things with the police. He agreed with Blaze. Xavier didn't want Mackie to go to jail for shooting him. Xavier wondered where Aleah had gone; he hadn't heard her voice. He didn't know why it sent him in such a rage knowing that she was messing around with Mackie's brother. He figured that she would always be at home waiting on him, until he decided that he was ready to call it quits on their marriage. Mackie had him considering ending his marriage to Aleah, but he felt that it was his choice not hers. He was the man of the house. He made the decisions. It was his and his alone.

When people tell you that they see their life flash before their eyes, Xavier could attest that to be true. He even saw the bright white light that people talked about. Xavier tried to run like hell from it. He wasn't ready to die. He had just started something with Mackie. He didn't know where it was heading, but he wanted a chance to find out.

Xavier heard Keya's voice when they removed him from the ambulance and rolled him into the emergency room. Keya was hysterical. Xavier tried his best open his eyes, but to no avail. He needed to console her as he has always done. "It's okay Keya. I'm here. I'll always be here for you." Xavier thought his words could be heard, but Keya wouldn't stop crying. Xavier strained to hear. He could hear Aleah now. Keya was asking her what happened. Keya sounded like she wanted to rip Aleah's head off. Xavier laughed. His sister the pit bull, was backing him up. He was still pissed at Aleah. He wanted Keya to tap that ass. All of a sudden, he couldn't hear anything anymore. Xavier shook his head. He could see their mouths moving but it was like he'd suddenly lost his hearing. Xavier wondered what was happening. Without warning, everything went dark. No lights, no voices, no thoughts. *Am I dead?*

Xavier was wheeled in for emergency surgery. The doctors cleaned the area around the wound to get a better look at the entry point and the direction that the bullet had traveled. They needed to stop the external bleeding before checking for any internal bleeding. After the bleeding was under control, checks would be made to see if any organs had been damaged.

The lead doctor left from the operating room to give Aleah an update on Xavier's condition. He walked into the waiting area and called, "Aleah Thomas."

Keya jumped up and crossed over to the doctor. "I'm Keya Thomas. Xavier is my brother. His wife had to step away for minute. Is he going to be ok?"

The doctor looked at Xavier's chart. He saw Keya's name listed as a relative. He wanted to make sure she was approved to receive information about Xavier's condition. Although she was listed, it didn't have her down as a person that could make decisions for him.

"I'm sorry. I can only provide information to his wife," the doctor informed her.

Keya was about to rip into the doctor, when her supervisor walked up. She had heard the doctor's response to Keya. She informed the doctor that Keya worked there at the hospital and that it would be okay to let her know what was happening with her brother.

Keya thanked her supervisor, before turning to the doctor to get the update on Xavier's condition.

"We are in the process of running tests to see what has been damaged. So far, we have injected arterial blood gases to determine his adequacy of oxygenation. We have checked his hemoglobin and hematocrit levels to give us an idea of any significant blood loss. We've ordered a chest x-ray to determine the extent of the injury. And also a CT of the upper torso to see if the wound extends into the chest cavity or spinal cord. We'll also be doing an MRI to evaluate any soft tissue injuries, foreign bodies, or hematomas. Lastly, we've ordered an ECG to detect any heart rhythm disturbances.

It was times like these that Keya was glad that she was a nurse. For anybody else, what the doctor was saying would have sounded like a bunch of gibberish, but not only did Keya know exactly what he was talking about, she knew in depth each procedure that would be conducted. This would be a long process, but she was determined to be right there for Xavier every step of the way. The only thing that she could do at this point would be to pray. After the doctor finished giving her the update, he went back into the operating room to continue working with the other doctors on Xavier.

Keya decided to go down to the chapel. It was a place that she could go lay her burdens down and ask the Lord to have mercy on Xavier's soul. She knew that Xavier hadn't been the ideal Christian, but she knew that he loved the Lord. She and Xavier hadn't been dealt the best hand when it came to fathers. She hoped God would be lenient knowing what experiences had shaped Xavier's personality. Keya knew that had their father not been abusive to them and their mother, Xavier would have never picked up those tendencies.

Keya knew that people responded to situations differently. She went through the same things as a child that Xavier did, but she had refused to become a violent person. Keya sat thinking about how she had behaved with Aleah. Aleah was her friend. She started to feel guilty for attacking her. She was like a sister to her. Aleah was right, she knew firsthand the hell that Xavier had put her through. Who was she to judge Aleah? Keya picked up her phone. She needed to call Aleah.

"Shit," she said. She'd forgotten that she had broken Aleah's phone. "Dammit." She dialed their house number, hoping that Aleah would pick up. It rang several times before going to voice mail.

CHAPTER SIX
BLAZE

Blaze was in the middle of explaining everything the detectives had said to his attorney when the detention officer knocked on the door.

"You have some more visitors," he said as he opened the door.

Aleah and Khalil walked in. Aleah went straight to Blaze and fell into his arms. He kissed her on the side of her face and hugged her tight. She didn't want to let go. He had become her knight in shining armor. Blaze pulled back a bit, looked in her eyes, and placed a soft kiss on Aleah's lips.

"Ok you two," Khalil interrupted.

Blaze stepped to the side and dapped Khalil. "Thanks man."

"You got it," Khalil responded.

"Blaze, I'm going to go work on your bail hearing. You've never been arrested and have never had even had a parking ticket. I don't foresee a problem with getting you bail," the attorney spoke.

"Let me know how much you need once it's been set," Khalil told him.

"Ok, I'll be in touch." The attorney tapped on the door letting the detention officer know that he was ready to leave.

"How's BJ?" Blaze asked Khalil.

"He's doing great. My mom is sitting with him. You know how much he loves my mom."

"Yeah, he really believes that she's his grandma," Blaze said.

"She is," Khalil stated. "And you're my brother from another mother."

"That's what's up," Blaze laughed. "Did Mackie make it to the house?"

"Yeah, I talked to Diesel earlier. She was pretty messed up but he calmed her down," Khalil explained.

"Cool, you know I want you to keep an eye on her. I know Diesel is going to do whatever he needs to do to protect her, but I would feel a whole lot better just knowing that you are watching over her too," Blaze told him.

"No doubt. I'll let y'all have a little privacy. Just meet me in the lobby when you're ready," he told Aleah.

"Ok, thanks," she responded.

Blaze sat down and pulled Aleah onto his lap. She laid her head on his chest. She wanted this entire ordeal to be over. She was afraid. Afraid for all of them; Xavier, Blaze, Keya, and Mackie. The next forty-eight hours would determine their futures. She wondered if their lie would stand up to the brutal questioning that would come in the bail hearing. And God forbid if they had to actually go to trial.

"Stop worrying," Blaze instructed.

"How do you know that I am worrying?" Aleah asked.

"It's written all over your face," he told her. "I may not have known you for a long time, but I know you. We have a connection," Blaze bragged.

"You think so, huh?" Aleah knew it too. She could feel it. It was unlike anything that she had ever felt with Xavier.

Blaze picked her up and repositioned her on his lap. She sat atop him, straddling his legs. Aleah's body immediately became inflamed. She felt Blaze's dick growing beneath her. She smiled. He knew she felt it. She started a slow rotation. Her hips dipped and rocked a slow grind. He gripped her ass encouraging her to continue. Blaze leaned forward keeping his eyes glued to Aleah's eyes. He leaned his mouth in, opening it, and used his teeth to ever so lightly clamp down on her nipple. A slight moan escaped Aleah's lips. Her head titled backwards as she enjoyed the sensation of Blaze teasing her nipple. He removed one hand from her ass and placed it on her breast. He squeezed sending her into overdrive.

"You'd better stop before I make you fuck me right here in this room," Aleah breathed.

Blaze laughed. "As much as I would love to do that, I don't want our first time to be in a funky ass interrogation room."

Blaze lifted her up off of his lap. Aleah straightened her blouse.

"Soon," he told her, "I'm going to show you how a real man loves a real woman."

Aleah's folds were dripping wet hearing Blaze speak about making love to her.

"Thank you for standing by me," Blaze said.

"It's the least I can do. You saved my life tonight. I saw the level of hate in Xavier's eyes tonight when he had me by the throat. If you hadn't gotten him off of me, I would be dead," Aleah believed.

Blaze pulled her into his arms again. He couldn't get enough of trying to love this woman. He'd kill a million men to keep her safe.

They turned towards the door when they heard a knock. The detention officer opened the door.

"Time's up," he told Blaze.

"I should be out of here some time tomorrow. As soon as I check on BJ and Mackie, I want to see you," Blaze said.

"I can't wait." Aleah kissed him on the lips and turned to walk from the room. She turned around and waved before disappearing down the long hallway. Before reaching the lobby, Aleah heard her name being called.

"Mrs. Thomas?" Aleah turned to see who she knew in the police station of all places.

"Fancy seeing you here," the detective said. He paused and looked down the hall to where they were walking Blaze back to the holding cell. He looked back at Aleah. "How's your husband?"

Aleah knew what he was implying. She couldn't care less. She was tired of trying to please everybody but herself. "He was still in surgery when I left," Aleah answered.

The detective looked at her blouse, remembering her boob hanging out. Aleah saw him staring at her breasts. When he licked his lips, Aleah folded her arms across her chest. He smiled.

"Don't hide it, divide it," the detective whispered. "I'm sure I could make you scream a whole lot louder than Blaze Carter."

Aleah tried to slap the detective, but his reflexes were quick. He grabbed her wrist.

"Hey, what's going on?" Khalil had stepped around the corner just as Aleah was about to slap the detective.

"Not much. The little lady is just a tad bit tired," he told Khalil.

"I guess I better get her home then," Khalil stepped in front of the detective.

Both men stood staring each other down. Khalil was 'bout it, 'bout it. If he ended up spending the night in jail for protecting what belonged to Blaze, then so be it.

"Guess you better," the detective responded and backed away.

"Are you ok?" Khalil asked Aleah.

"Yes, thank you."

"Come on. Let's get out of here." Khalil escorted Aleah from the station and to his car.

Aleah had Khalil to stop her by the AT&T store so that she could replace her phone. When she got back into his car, she called the hospital to check on Xavier's condition. The nurse told her that he was still in surgery. Aleah had Khalil to drop her off at home. She wanted to shower, change clothes and pick up her own car.

Once Aleah finished with everything, she hopped in her car and headed towards the hospital. She didn't want to do a round two with Keya, but she felt like she needed to check on Xavier in person. If for nothing else, she needed to keep up with appearance's sake. She didn't want the police wondering why she wasn't there to see about her husband.

CHAPTER SEVEN
KEYA

Keya wondered where Aleah had gone. She knew she didn't have her car. She had arrived at the hospital in the ambulance with Xavier. She didn't remember seeing her with her purse either, so chances were that she did not have money to take a cab or ride the bus. Keya smiled thinking that it would be something to see Aleah's prissy ass riding the city bus.

"She has to be still in the hospital somewhere," Keya stated. "Guess I'll go find her."

Keya walked out of the chapel and began her search. She looked in every waiting room on every floor that she could think of. Aleah was in none of them. She checked he cafeteria. Aleah was definitely not in the hospital.

Keya wasn't ready to give up her search just yet. "Maybe she decided to get some fresh air."

Keya walked back to the front of the hospital. She'd decided to check the benches just outside the foyer.

"Miss Thomas?" she heard her name being called.

Keya turned in the direction of the man's voice.

"Detective," Keya stated.

"How is it going?" he asked.

"As well as can be expected," she answered.

"Is your brother still in surgery?" he asked.

"Yes, I am hoping that's a good thing," Keya said.

"That's what his wife said," the detective stated, fully well intending to get a rise out of Keya.

"Have you seen her, Aleah?" she asked.

"Oh yes, I saw her down at the station a little while ago."

"At the station," Keya seethed.

"Yes, she was there visiting her friend Blaze Carter." The detective waited for the fireworks. It was a tactic that he employed all the time. Get people angry and they start to tell you things that they hadn't meant to say.

"That bitch," Keya growled.

"Do you know Blaze Carter?" he asked.

"No, I don't know that son of bitch," Keya spewed. "But I did meet him when his son came in with a gunshot wound."

The detective perked up. *Just the kind of information that I'm looking for,* he thought. He pulled out his recorder and pressed play. Keya was so caught up in her rant that she hadn't noticed.

"I'm sure that bullet was meant for him or sister. That little boy was just an innocent bystander. When you sell drugs for a living, you put everybody that you know in harm's way."

"Are you saying that Blaze Carter is a drug dealer?"

"That's exactly what I'm saying. Him and his sister Mackie," Keya continued.

"Blaze and Mackie Carter," he prodded.

Something clicked in Keya's mind as she realized the detective was just trying to get information out of her. He wasn't concerned about her or Xavier.

Keya was about to go off on him, when they both turned to the sound of Aleah's voice.

"Hey," she said wondering what she was walking up on. She had clearly heard the detective say Blaze and Mackie Carter.

"Oh, so you decided to come back after you went to see your little boyfriend?" Keya spat.

Aleah's head whipped towards the detective. He shrugged his shoulders.

"What, you thought he was going to keep your secret?" Keya added.

"It wasn't a secret," Aleah sighed.

"Oh, so now you are admitting that you are having an affair with Blaze Carter?"

"That's not what I was saying," Aleah said.

"Are you or are you not fucking Blaze?" Keya demanded. She was pissed that Aleah was possibly cheating on Xavier, but she was also pissed because she had been attracted to Blaze herself. She was being a bitch to him but that was more to get him to want her. She didn't know how she felt about Blaze after she found out that he was a drug dealer, but now that Aleah was probably fucking him, that left her as the third wheel once again.

"No, I am not fucking him," Aleah answered truthfully.

"But you are seeing him?" Keya asked.

"That's not what's important right now," Aleah stated.

"Spoken like a person who wants to avoid the conversation," the detective budded in.

"This has nothing to do with you," Aleah yelled at him.

"Don't take you frustration about getting busted out on him!" Keya was relentless.

"I'm just saying, you two seemed pretty cozy when I peeped into the interrogation room," the detective added.

Aleah wanted to kick him in his balls. Keya turned an entirely different shade.

"Here I was feeling sorry for fighting with you earlier. I was actually looking for you to apologize. You are a fucking sneaky ass hoe. No wonder Xavier was kicking your ass, you weak ass bitch," Keya said.

Keya knew she shouldn't have said that. It had been rough for Aleah putting up with Xavier physically abusing her. She had so many emotions running through her body right now that she wasn't thinking clearly. If Xavier died and Aleah started a new life with Blaze, where would that leave her?

Tears streaked Aleah's face. She considered Keya her sister, best friend and confidant. *How can you turn on me so easily?* she thought.

"I can't believe you just said that to me. You better than anybody else know the hell that Xavier has put me through. When a man shows a little interest in me, I would think that you of all people would ask me about it first rather than accusing me."

Keya was livid. Aleah had just said that Blaze was interested in her.

"Let's get something straight. Xavier is my first and only concern. Xavier may be a little flawed, but he loves you," Keya said.

"Oh, he loves me, huh?" Aleah reached in her purse pulling out her new phone. She scrolled to her email, glad she had sent the video to herself. She pressed play and held up the recording of Xavier and Mackie having sex on the balcony.

Keya covered her mouth with her hand.

The detective moved in closer. "Damn," he said as he looked at Mackie's ass hanging over the railing.

"You sick son of a bitch," Aleah said to him.

Aleah turned back to Keya. "Xavier is not innocent at all, so you can stop trying to make me out as the villain. I have put up with him beating the shit out of me since I married him. I will not put up with him screwing other women too."

Aleah was still holding the phone up so that Keya could see it. She finally clicked the phone off.

"I'm going to need to get a copy of that," the detective said.

Both Aleah and Keya looked at him and frowned.

"Fuck you," Aleah said as she turned to walk away.

"Aleah," Keya called.

"Save it!" Aleah walked back out of the front door of the hospital.

CHAPTER EIGHT
MACKIE

Mackie slept peacefully knowing that Diesel was there with her. Diesel on the other hand didn't get a wink of sleep. His dick stayed hard half the night. Every time he got close to dozing off, Mackie would shift in the bed and reposition some part of her body on his. Her ass pressed into his crotch and her breasts resting on his chest, both kept him hot and bothered.

Diesel wondered about this new guy that Mackie was seeing. Khalil had called to fill him on everything when he got to the house yesterday. Most of the guys that Mackie dealt with didn't cause any concern for Diesel. He knew she was just getting a little quick fix to tide her over. But this Xavier guy had indirectly caused her to feel, when no one else could.

He hated that Mackie had opened herself up to be hurt like this. He couldn't remember one single time that Mackie had cried. Diesel wanted to seriously put a hurting on Xavier, but Khalil told him that Blaze said that everyone needed to lay low until this situation was over. They were all going to have an extra set of eyes on them for a while. Khalil was handling things with the operation. He suspended all shipments until further notice. Diesel thought it was an overkill, but decided not to voice his opinion. His judgment had been off point lately. He knew it was because of his growing feelings for Mackie.

Shay had called early this morning, asking when he was going to come by. He had to again tell her that he wasn't sure. Of course she was pissed.

"I'm sick of coming second to that bitch," Shay barked into the phone at Diesel.

Mackie was laying on Diesel's chest at the time. She had heard the phone when it rang, but pretended to be still asleep. She heard Shay clearly call her a bitch. Mackie was pissed but didn't let on that she had heard.

Mackie didn't give a shit about Shay. If she felt like Shay really loved Diesel, she would encourage him to spend more time with her but she knew what Shay was all about. *Just for that*, Mackie thought, *I am going to keep him all day.*

When Diesel hung up the phone, Mackie started stirring a bit. Diesel wished she would be still. Every time she moved while she was laying on his chest, he felt the softness of her breasts. It felt so damn good to him. Mackie had huge plump breasts with big nipples. Diesel would sneak glances when he could; not on purpose, he just couldn't help it. He knew that Mackie had seen him on more than one occasion, but she never said anything about it.

Mackie loved lying on Diesel's chest. Diesel was a big man with a solid build. Mackie talked shit to Diesel all the time, but she had no doubt that he could put her on her ass if he wanted to. No matter what Mackie did or said, he was team Mackie. She had the best of both worlds with him: a bodyguard and a best friend.

Mackie opened her eyes and looked up at him.

Even just waking up she's gorgeous, Diesel thought.

"Good morning," Mackie spoke.

"Morning," Diesel answered.

"What happened to the good?" Mackie teased.

I'm hard as a rock, got pussy laying on me and can't dip into it, he wanted to say.

Mackie moved her head further up into the crook of Diesel's arm and snuggled in closer. She was now lying next to him.

Mackie had a clear view of the rise in the sheet between Diesel's legs. She shook her head, *is he always horny?*

Here Shay was bitching and he still had an erection. Mackie abruptly sat up. It was like a light bulb going off in her head. She turned to look at Diesel. His eyes were closed. He was doing those breathing exercises again.

She wondered if Diesel had a thing for her.

"Diesel," Mackie called.

He opened his eyes. "What's up?"

"Nothing," she answered. If he did have romantic feelings for her, she didn't want to know. Diesel was handsome, but there was no way that she would taint their friendship just to have them at each other's throats when things didn't work out.

Mackie stood and walked to the bathroom, looking back at Diesel. She saw it in his eyes. He wanted her. Mackie closed the door and leaned against it. She sighed. Her life was being turned upside down. *Am I getting too old for this shit?*

Mackie stood under the warm water, allowing the feeling of the sprinkles to relieve her stress. She needed to do a whole lot of soul searching. She needed to figure out a way to get back to herself. Gangsta Mackie was missing in action. There was so much going on with her and Blaze right now that she wondered how the empire was still standing. *Khalil and Diesel*, she quickly surmised. *Without those two...* Mackie let her thoughts trail off.

Mackie reluctantly turned off the shower and stepped from her conclave. When she did, she heard the voices of two men talking. She immediately wrapped herself in a towel and reached into the drawer of the vanity to pull her piece. She leaned against the door, placing her ear to it. After listening for a half second, she swung the door opened and squealed.

Mackie crossed the room with the speed of a jack rabbit. She leapt into Blaze's arms almost knocking him down. Blaze and Diesel laughed.

"Something is seriously wrong with you," Blaze told her. "Who takes a shower with their gun?"

"Queen Mackie," Diesel joked.

"Dealing with wanna be gangstas and cracked out hoes, you can never be too careful," she told them.

Mackie was still dripping wet. She hadn't dried off. The towel was only haphazardly secured around her waist. If it was to fall, Diesel would be no good.

"I'm going to get a little air… give you two a chance to talk in private," Diesel explained.

"Thanks Diesel," Blaze said, "for everything!"

"You got it," Diesel answered.

Diesel left the room, *and none too soon*, he thought. He needed to add a little space between him and Mackie. Literally. He had done well suppressing his feelings for Mackie for such a long time now. He wondered why now, he was having a hard time controlling his emotions. After thinking for a while, he figured it might be because she actually seemed to be really interested in Xavier.

CHAPTER NINE
BLAZE

Blaze was just as happy to see Mackie. Khalil had told him that she was fine but it was nothing like seeing it for yourself. He could tell that Mackie had cried a lot. To everyone else she might look normal, but he knew. Her eyes were still just a tad bit puffy.

Blaze had decided not to tell Mackie everything that happened yesterday. He didn't want her to worry about the agents that had come to see him at the station. Knowing his sister, she would probably try to take both of them out. That's one thing that Blaze didn't want to do, was get into a pissing contest with the FBI or DEA. He was smart enough to know that they had far more power than the Carter family alone.

"How is Xavier?" Mackie asked.

"I haven't heard anything today, but last night he was still in surgery when I talked to Aleah."

"Can you text her now to ask her how he is doing?"

Blaze pulled out his phone and sent a quick text to Aleah asking about Xavier. Personally, Blaze could care less if Xavier lived or died. *He abused his wife and then cheated on her with Mackie. Xavier ain't got shit coming from me or Mackie, if I can help it,* he thought.

"What happened yesterday?" Mackie asked Blaze.

Blaze went through a detailed rerun of what had happened when Mackie went to the store.

"I knew Xavier was married," Mackie whispered. "Does that make me a bad person?"

"No," Blaze answered. "I knew Aleah was married."

"What?" Mackie said surprised. Mackie couldn't believe that Blaze had known that Aleah was married. It wasn't a part of his character. She, on the other hand, had made dating married men a hobby. It was just easier for everyone involved, except for the wife. And even that was up in the air. Mackie felt like on the other hand, she was helping wives out. It was one less time that they had to sex their husbands' crazy after a long day of work and dealing with the kids.

"I had no clue that her husband was Xavier," Blaze acknowledged.

"I want to see him."

"Why?" Blaze was irritated.

Mackie didn't answer.

"I don't think that's a good idea," Blaze responded.

"Why?" Mackie wanted to know.

"I don't want you anywhere near this case," Blaze answered.

"Blaze, I have to see him. I need to know that he's alright. I want him to know that I didn't mean to shoot him. I mean, I didn't know it was him. I just wanted to get whoever it was off of you," Mackie rambled.

"Mackie, I know but it's way too risky. The police are hanging around the hospital and asking questions to any and everybody they can. If someone remembers that you have been spending time with him, they will have even more questions. More questions for us means more lies, and that could lead to our story unraveling," Blaze told her.

Mackie was clearly pouting. Blaze didn't care this time. Normally, he would give in to her when she threw a tantrum, but this time he knew what he needed to do to keep her safe, and no amount of lips stuck out was going to change that.

"As a matter of fact," Blaze continued, "I think it might be a good idea for you to get out of town for a little while."

"Out of town?" Mackie repeated his words.

"At least until this thing blows over."

"I am not leaving town," Mackie stated. "What if something happens with Xavier?"

"Diesel can go with you and I can keep you both updated on what's happening back here."

At the mention of Diesel's name, Mackie tensed. Blaze noticed.

"Everything cool with you and Diesel?" Blaze asked.

"Yeah, why did you ask that?"

"Mackie, I can read you like a book. When I mentioned his name just now, you tensed. And right now, you seem out of sorts. Do I need to handle his ass?"

"No, and lower your voice," Mackie told him.

"Well you better start talking."

"I think he might have a thing for me," Mackie admitted.

"Diesel has always had a thing for you Mackie."

"What?" Mackie yell whispered.

Blaze laughed. "You mean to tell me you didn't know?"

"No, and why didn't you tell me? And how do you know? Did he say something to you about me?"

"Damn girl, which question do you want me to answer first?" Blaze asked.

"All of them!"

"No, he didn't say anything to me. It was just the way he looks at you when he thinks no one else is watching. And I didn't say anything because I wasn't one-hundred percent sure," Blaze answered. "So how do you feel about him? "

Mackie frowned. "Diesel is like a brother to me."

"I am your one and only brother."

"I said like a brother, fool," Mackie said.

"But he's not, so I don't see a reason as to why you couldn't date him." Blaze was sounding like he was pro Diesel. This would be a win-win for Blaze. Mackie would be with someone that he knew and someone that could watch her back. And he thought, *Diesel would keep her away from the wife beater.*

"Blaze, I will not take dating advice from you. And if you are encouraging me to date somebody, then that's the last person that I want to be with," Mackie stated.

"And why is that?" Blaze was offended.

"Because that will mean that you can keep up with everything that I do, no thank you."

"You already have Khalil snapping pictures of me and shit when I'm not looking," Mackie laughed.

"All I'm saying is that Diesel is one-hundred. He'd do anything for you. You need a man that wants to love and protect only you."

"Oh, how sweet," Mackie mocked. "But you do know that Diesel is heavy in the game, right? I thought you wanted me dating a nice college educated man. And besides all that, Diesel is in a relationship with Shay and they have a kid. I am not trying to bust up his happy home."

"I did want that for you, but Diesel has really proved to me that he would care for you just as I would. And Shay is a trashy, money hungry bitch. Everybody knows that but Diesel."

'If for some reason I am not around, I know that he would hold you down."

"What do you mean if you're not around?" Mackie asked. "Why would you say that?"

"No reason. I'm just thinking out loud."

"Blaze, we are always going to be together. But you don't have to worry about me. I am fully capable of taking care of myself," Mackie said.

Yeah right, Blaze thought. "I'm just saying, don't be so quick to count Diesel out. This thing with Xavier might just be temporary. Diesel is long term."

"Whatever," Mackie stated.

When Blaze's phone buzzed, Mackie jumped up and reached for it, but Blazed moved away from her reach.

"Let me see. What did she say?" Mackie asked.

"She said she left the hospital after getting into it with Xavier's sister, Keya. She's been calling the hospital talking to the nurses. She said the surgery went well. But he hasn't regained consciousness yet."

"That's good, right?" she asked Blaze.

Blaze wanted to say 'hell no'. Xavier could be the one person to bring down the entire operation. If he wakes up and tells the police that Mackie was the one that shot him, she will be the one that's facing prison time. Mackie is not thinking straight and hasn't been since she met him.

"Is that it? What else did she say?" Mackie asked.

"She said Mackie Carter needs to run like hell in the opposite direction of Xavier Thomas," Blazed laughed, but was serious as a heart attack.

"Quit playing." Mackie said it in a happy voice, but until she had a chance to talk with Xavier, she'd be on pins and needles wondering if he hated her for shooting him or not.

Blaze stood up. "I need to get to the hospital to check on BJ. Khalil's mom stayed with him last night. She said he's been asking for us.

"I'm going with you," Mackie said.

"Mackie, you can't go with me," Blaze responded.

"Why, I want to see BJ?"

"Not until this thing with Xavier is over. When I get there, I'll FaceTime you and you can talk to him."

Mackie sighed. She knew that Blaze wasn't going to budge on this one.

"Fine," she pouted. "Can you check on Xavier while you're there?"

Blaze sighed. He had no interest in seeing Xavier or Keya. If Keya lit into Aleah, he could just imagine the words that she had for him.

"Sure," he finally answered.

CHAPTER TEN
ALEAH

Aleah jumped up from the bed after letting out a scream that she was sure woke up the neighborhood. Sweat was dripping from her forehead. She looked around trying to remember where she was. She breathed in and out at a fast pace, trying to take in as much air as possible.

She had been dreaming. Xavier hands were once again around her neck, squeezing the life out of her body. As much as she tried, she couldn't pry his hands off of her. This time Blaze nor Mackie came to her rescue.

Aleah finally remembered where she was. Khalil had given her keys and the address to one of Blaze's houses if she needed a place to stay for a while. Initially, she had said she wouldn't use it, but after the incident with Keya at the hospital, she didn't want to go home and chance running into her again.

Aleah thought about what Keya had said about Blaze and Mackie. She wondered if it was true. Were they drug dealers? Thinking about their house last night and the house that she was in now, *it was possible*, she thought.

Aleah wasn't sure how she felt about that. Blaze had told her that he was an entrepreneur. "Technically, he didn't lie," she said.

Aleah had always followed the law. Blaze seemed so normal. He was kind and sweet. Drug dealers are mean and ruthless. It didn't make sense to her. There had to be some other explanation.

Aleah was nervous at first, entering the home and walking around it. She'd grabbed a bat from the closet by the front door. She had half expected someone to jump out and attack her. The house looked normal. It was fully furnished and clothes were hanging in all the closets and folded in all the drawers. She could tell which room was Blaze's, Mackie's and BJ's. Each had their own distinctive style. The home wasn't as large as the home from last night, but it was still nice. It was larger than her and Xavier's three-bedroom home.

Although there was a guest room, Aleah decided to sleep in Blaze's bed. She somehow felt more protected in his room. She found a large t-shirt to sleep in. She'd showered with both the bedroom and bathroom doors locked.

Aleah cried her eyes out in the comfort of the shower. She had no clue what she was doing or where this all would end. She was married to a cheating monster, while attracted to a drug dealer. She was more than attracted to Blaze. Aleah wanted to spend every moment of every day getting to know him. She was sure everyone back home would be shocked beyond belief if they knew how her life had turned out.

"What a joke I am," she cried. All Aleah could do was climb into the oversized bed when she got out of the shower. She was truly worn out. She was sure her eyes closed and she was off to sleep, even before her head hit the pillow.

The sound of her own screaming had scared the shit out of her. It seemed so real. Xavier was only a few minutes from sending her into the afterlife.

Aleah climbed out of the bed. The house was as quite as a mausoleum. She was again nervous, but not as much as last night because the sunlight was glimmering through the windows. Aleah unlocked the bedroom door and began exploring the house once again. The home was even more beautiful now that she could actually see. It was a home that Aleah could see herself living in. It reminded her of her childhood home. Her parents had normal jobs, but both were supervisors earning a combined salary well into six figures.

Aleah peeked from the front window. She knew where this neighborhood was but not this particular subdivision. It was hidden behind another subdivision up a long winding big hill. It was definitely a place that people wouldn't know was there. Aleah thought she was lost driving up the road and was about to turn around when she saw the first home. The homes were spaced out with lots of yard.

Aleah was surprised when she looked into the refrigerator. It was fully stocked. Nothing was expired. Aleah wondered if Mackie had gone shopping. Had she planned on bringing Xavier here? Aleah was getting pissed all over again. Mackie seemed nice. "Maybe she didn't know that Xavier was married. Men do lie," she said.

Aleah decided to call the hospital again to check on Xavier. When she had called last night, they'd told her that he was out of surgery, had been given a room and was resting. The nurse gave her the same spill that she had last night. Aleah hung up the phone and thought about Blaze. She smiled without realizing it. As if on cue, her phone rang and Blaze's name flashed across her screen. She'd saved it in her phone the night she saw Xavier and Mackie fucking on the balcony.

"Hello," Aleah said into the phone.

"Hey beautiful," Blaze spoke.

"You've been released?" Aleah asked.

"Yeah, about an hour ago I posted bond. I've got a brand spanking new ankle monitor as a get out jail gift. Where are you?" Blazed questioned.

"I'm at your house," Aleah told him.

"Which one?"

"In Frost Farms," Aleah answered. "Where are you?"

"I just left Mackie. I'm on my way to the hospital to see BJ."

At the sound of Blaze mentioning Mackie, Aleah got quiet. She had so many questions. The only problem was that she wasn't so sure she wanted to know the answers.

"Aleah," Blaze had called her name for the third time.

"Huh?" Aleah mumbled.

"Are you ok?" Blazed was concerned.

"Yes, I'm good."

"I can't wait to see you," Blaze stated. "I missed you."

Aleah was back fully paying attention. Those words were soothing to her soul. "I missed you too. I can't wait to see you," Aleah smiled.

"As soon as I make sure that BJ is ok, I'm coming home to you."

Aleah loved the sound of that. "Ok," she giggled.

"Do you mind if I cook for you?" Aleah asked.

"I would love for you to cook for me. Just know that I have a greedy appetite," Blaze stated, hoping that Aleah caught his play on words. "I want to taste everything that you've got."

"Are you being naughty?" Aleah wanted to tease.

"Damn right," Blaze answered.

"Everything I got is simmering for you right now."

"Keep it warm for me," Blaze added.

"Absolutely," Aleah told him.

CHAPTER ELEVEN
KEYA

Keya spent the night in Xavier's room. She never realized how uncomfortable the chairs were in the rooms. She had brought covers and pillows to tons of patients over the last few years. Now she was the one that snuggled in a too little chair, with a rough heavy blanket and a too soft pillow, waiting on her loved one to get better.

It had taken Keya hours to fall asleep. The stress of everything hadn't allowed her the opportunity to relax. Xavier came out of surgery around midnight. But it wasn't until almost 2am that Keya finally dozed off to sleep. Even then, it was hard to get any sleep with the nurses coming in every hour. As soon as she was getting a little deeper into her sleep, the door would open. Light from the hallway would slap Keya in the face every time. Xavier wasn't bothered one bit. He was still heavily sedated. The hospital could be burning down and he wouldn't know it.

Keya stood to stretch. Her body was sore from being cramped into that chair all night. She looked over at Xavier. She felt bad for him. He hadn't had the best in life, neither had she. But surely they could pull their lives back together. Keya didn't know if Xavier and Aleah's marriage could be saved, or even if either of them still wanted to try to save their marriage. But she certainly didn't want him with Mackie.

As much as Keya didn't want to think about Aleah, she did. Aleah had been her bestie for so long, it was hard to stay mad at her.

Everything that Aleah was saying was true. She had put up with so much shit from Xavier that it was a wonder that she hadn't left his ass a long time ago. Nonetheless, knowing that Aleah had something to do with Xavier being shot, made her angry.

Keya thought about Blaze and how much she was attracted to him. She had honestly considered dating him. She could still feel his breath on her neck the day he stood behind her in his son's room. She thought for sure that he wanted her. *Guess he was just being a man*, she thought. "He wants Aleah," she stated. A sadness engulfed her. She was single and attractive. Aleah was married and yet, he still wanted her. "What's wrong with me?" she whispered.

Keya stepped over to Xavier's bed. "I'm going downstairs to get some coffee." She kissed him on his forehead before leaving the room.

As she walked down to the cafeteria, she was stopped several times by her co-workers asking how Xavier was doing. Keya was thankful for the well wishes and prayers that most gave. She was starting to feel more alone each passing minute. It truly was just her and Xavier. Life was funny. Keya had thought that she and Aleah would be friends for life. One incident tore them apart. Even if Xavier and Aleah stayed together, things would never be the same again.

Keya got her coffee and was walking back up to Xavier's room, when she couldn't believe her eyes. She could have sworn that she saw Blaze walking into his son's room. *Maybe my eyes are playing tricks on me,* she thought. He's supposed to be in jail; still locked up for shooting Xavier.

Keya picked up her pace, ignoring everyone that tried to speak to her. She reached the door to BJ's room and peeked through the window. "That bastard," she said. She watched as Blaze smiled and laughed with his son. She paid no attention to the other people in the room. When Blaze looked up, he saw Keya looking through the window.

"Damn," he whispered. He didn't feel like dealing with her attitude right now. He just wanted to spend a little time enjoying BJ.

Khalil looked over to see what had Blaze's attention. "Who's that?" he asked. He could see in her facial expression that she was pissed off.

"Keya, Xavier's sister," Blaze told him.

"Oh," Khalil responded. "Do you want me to handle it?"

"Yeah, but be easy with her," Blaze instructed. "I think she's a nice girl, just needs a little dick in her life."

"Alright," Khalil answered as he stood.

He walked to the door opening. Keya tried to sidestep him but he blocked her path with his body.

"Get out of my way," Keya yelled.

"I can't. Blaze is busy with his son right now," Khalil told her.

"I don't give a shit," Keya told him. "Who the fuck do you think you are Blaze? You fucking shoot my brother last night and already out."

Khalil wasn't going to allow her to continue to curse like a sailor in front of the kids. His son was also in the room visiting with BJ. He was glad that he had sent his mother home this morning. The last thing she needed to hear was that Blaze had shot somebody.

Khalil lifted Keya off the ground with one swift motion. He'd picked her up like a baby.

The cup of coffee spilled all over Khalil. He winced at the feel of the hot liquid as it made contact with his skin. Keya didn't care. Her goal was getting to Blaze.

"Put me down," she repeated.

Khalil ignored her demands until he reached a vacant room. He walked into the room and sat her down on the bed. He closed the door and told her he wasn't going to let her leave the room until she calmed down.

"So you're his fucking stooge. Do you sell drugs too?" she vented. "I guess you shoot innocent people too," she added.

Khalil listened to her ramble and rage in her thoughts for at least fifteen minutes. When he felt like she was starting to calm down he spoke.

"Keya," right.

"Yeah," she answered.

"My name is Khalil."

"Nice name, I was expecting something like Bullet or Mad Dog," Keya said.

Khalil laughed.

Keya smiled. She was still pissed off but decided not to waste her energy on Blaze. She needed to stay focused on Xavier and his recovery.

"Look, I don't know what you have heard about Blaze, but most people have him pegged wrong. He's genuine."

"Of course you are going to say that, you work for him," Keya said.

"I do work for him, but it's more than that. I am highly sought after. Everybody wants me on their team but I chose to work for the Carter's mainly because of Blaze. And I'll tell you this, for him to shoot your brother, he absolutely would have had to have no choice. Blaze doesn't do guns. He thinks that using guns is a coward's way out. I don't know what all happened last night, but Blaze is a good dude."

"That's a damn oxymoron; a good drug dealer," Keya stated.

"May be, but it's the truth.

"Yeah, well what about Mack Bitch?" Keya asked, remembering what her friend told her about how ruthless Mackie was.

Khalil laughed at Keya using the nickname that dealers on the street had given to Mackie. "Mackie is very different from Blaze. But she wasn't dealt the best hand in life. She's gone through some things that have had a negative effect on her personality." Khalil just left it at that. He didn't want to tell Keya that Mackie had shot and killed her mother when she was just a little girl. *That would fuck anybody up*, Khalil thought.

Keya's mind went into overdrive. She wanted to know details. What had screwed Mackie up so bad that she had the heart of a gangsta?

CHAPTER TWELVE
MACKIE

Mackie was bored shitless. Being cooped up in the house was not something that she was used to. Since she was able to drive, she never stayed at home over two hours unless she was asleep.

Diesel had been arguing back and forth with Shay all morning. Mackie eavesdropped on his conversation for a while, but even that got boring to her. She didn't understand why Blaze wanted to keep her in the house and away from Xavier. Nobody even knew that she was at the house last night.

"Hey, are you hungry?" Diesel asked.

"Yes, let's go out to eat," Mackie got excited.

"We can't go out. Well, you can't go out. I was going to go pick up something for us. Blaze doesn't want you to leave the house," Diesel told her.

"You don't work for Blaze!" Mackie was pissed.

"Please don't do this Mackie."

Mackie softened her attitude. It was something about him saying *please Mackie* that touched her heart. In that moment, she saw something in Diesel that she hadn't seen before. She couldn't put her finger on it, but she was touched in a way that was different. It was something that she didn't want to feel.

Shit, Mackie thought. *I have to get out of this freaking house.*

"Fine," Mackie conceded.

"What do you want to eat?"

Mackie's mind was moving a mile a minute. "I want a baked potato from H&J's."

"H&J's," Diesel repeated. "That's all the way over in Oak Cliff."

"I know where it is. But you did ask me what I wanted," Mackie replied.

"Alright," Diesel told her.

Mackie was sending him to Oak Cliff on purpose. It would take him at least an hour to get there and back. As soon as his car cut the corner, she planned to hop in her own car, rush over to the hospital, peek in on Xavier and rush back before Diesel got back. *When he's on his way back, I'll ask him to stop at Braum's to pick up some ice cream.*

"Thank you Diesel," Mackie sang.

"Whatever," he replied.

Diesel grabbed his keys and walked out the front door. Mackie grabbed a cap off the coatrack and peeped out the window. She watched as Diesel backed his car out of the driveway. She opened the front door when he started down the street. Once she saw the car turn the corner, she ran to her car, climbed in and took off.

Mackie was careful to drive the speed limit. The last thing that she wanted was to get pulled over by the police for speeding. Blaze would have a conniption fit. She called the hospital on the drive over to get Xavier's room number. She hoped that God was smiling down on her so that she wouldn't run into Blaze or Keya. Fifteen minutes later, she was pulling her car into a parking space at the hospital. She pulled the cap down low to cover her eyes, and put her shades on. It would be hard for anybody to know who she was with a cap and glasses on.

Mackie got out of the car and quickly walked into the hospital. She decided to take the stairs up to Xavier's room. She figured there would be much less traffic in the stairwell than people riding on the elevator. Mackie sprinted up the stairs. She hadn't worked out this morning, so she welcomed the chance to get her heart rate up. Mackie stuck her head out of the stairwell, looking up and down the hallway.

Yes, she thought. Not a soul in sight. Mackie made it to Xavier's room. She looked inside before entering. "God is definitely smiling down on me," Mackie whispered. Keya was nowhere in sight.

Mackie walked into the room and stood next to Xavier's bed. A tear fell from Mackie's eye. Xavier looked bad. He looked much worse than BJ had when he came out of surgery. Mackie wondered why he had so many tubes connected to his body. The breathing machine was making an awful sound as it pumped air into Xavier.

Mackie reached down placing her hand into Xavier's hand. "Hey," she whispered. "It's me, Mackie." Mackie could have sworn she felt Xavier squeeze her hand.

Mackie turned towards the door as it swung open with force.

"What the fuck are you doing in here?" Keya screamed. Khalil had managed to calm her down, but it was short lived. When she looked into the window and saw Mackie standing over Xavier, she went ballistic.

"Mackie, what are you doing here?" Khalil asked.

"I had to see if he was alright for myself," Mackie answered.

"No, you came to try to finish him off for your brother," Keya barked.

"That's not true."

"Yes it is bitch, but I'll fuck you up before I let you do anything to him," Keya continue.

Khalil knew he had to get control of this situation. Keya had no idea who she was fucking with. He knew Mackie's temper and at any moment, if she kept coming at Mackie like she was, Mackie was going to reach out and touch her. And it wasn't going to be pretty.

"I came to check on Xavier. He just squeezed my hand when I was talking to him," Mackie stated.

"You're a damned liar," Keya spit. "I'm calling the police so they can arrest your ass for coming in here uninvited. It's called trespassing bitch. All of them niggas out on the street might be scared of your ass, but I'm not. You and your punk ass brother are going to jail."

That was it. Before Khalil knew what was happening Mackie had moved with the quickness of lightening and slapped the shit out Keya. Keya was in a state of shock. She hit the floor with a loud thump. When she realized that Mackie had just slapped her, she jumped up and charged at Mackie. Mackie laid her ass out flat on the floor. Mackie was about to pounce on her, when lights and beeps started sounding off like it was a kid's party going on. The machines that were attached to Xavier were giving off alerts.

Khalil pushed Mackie to the door. "Get the hell out of here now." He had never talked to Mackie in this tone before. It got her attention. She hated to leave right now. Something was happening with Xavier. "Go," Khalil said to her again.

Mackie ran from the room and back into the stairwell. As she rushed away, nurses and doctors ran in to see what was happening with Xavier.

By the time that Mackie reached the parking lot, she was bawling. She hadn't meant for any of this to happen. She just wanted to see Xavier. Mackie hit the stirring wheel. "I can't stand that bitch. How the fuck is she Xavier's sister? He's nothing like her." Mackie started the car and drove away. She hoped that Khalil wouldn't tell Blaze what had just happened.

CHAPTER THIRTEEN
XAVIER

Xavier had tried his best to open his eyes. He knew the moment that Mackie had walked into his room. He could feel her presence. Then he smelled her scent. It was a scent that he had fallen in love with. The excitement that he felt knowing that she had come to see him, made him happy.

He squeezed her hand to let her know that he could hear her. He had so many things that he wanted to say to her, but it was like his entire body was paralyzed. The words were forming in his head, but never made it to his mouth. Xavier knew that he wanted Mackie in his life. He and Aleah were done, he'd decided. Even if Mackie didn't want him, he didn't want to continue in a loveless marriage. Especially one that made him want to be violent. Mackie soothed him. He wanted to be everything that she wanted in man, a husband. But if she wasn't that person, he was sure that she was out there somewhere waiting for him. Life had to be more than what he'd been experiencing. Surely God didn't create us to live in such turmoil. *I want to be happy, I am going to choose to be happy,* he thought.

Xavier heard the minute that Keya came into the room. *She was wrong. Mackie cared about me. She didn't know that it was me that she was shooting.* But Keya wouldn't listen. It was the one thing that he hated about his sister. She would run off at the mouth without listening to what the other person was trying to say.

Stop it, shut up. Keya. The words were loud and clear in his head. "Either they can't hear me or they are ignoring me," Xavier said. Xavier heard a man's voice as he tried to control the situation. He was failing. Xavier heard a smack and a thud. He struggled to raise up. He needed to see what was going on. Xavier struggled. It was like he was at war with his own body. Then the pain. The pain pierced through his body unlike anything he had ever felt before. The pain was worse than the pain he experienced when the bullet tore through the flesh in his back. Everything suddenly went dark. Quiet.

"What's happening?" Keya cried. Khalil was right next to her with his hand on her back. "Xavier," she called.

"I'm sorry but we need you to step out of the room," the nurse instructed.

"No," Keya said.

"Keya," the nurse called her by her name. "Please let us help your brother."

Keya hadn't realized that it was her friend that was there working to stabilize Xavier. She nodded her head and allowed Khalil to lead her from the room.

After they exited the room, Khalil tried his best to make her believe that everything was going to be alright. He wasn't sure, but knew that was what he was supposed to say.

Keya's cries didn't stop. He reached out to pull her into an embrace. She allowed him to console her. She rested her head on his chest and let her emotions continue to flow.

Blaze rounded the corner. He had wondered what was taking Khalil so long. Khalil's mother had returned and they both were wondering what was keeping him. Blaze was glad that Keya's back was turned towards him. He looked at Khalil and mouthed the words "What's up?"

Khalil mouthed back "call Mackie." Blaze nodded his head. He watched as doctors and nurses moved in and out of Xavier's room. When the door opened, he could see in and hear what was happening.

"We need to resuscitate," a doctor called out.

Blaze knew that this meant Xavier had stopped breathing. They were going to send electric shocks to his heart muscle until it started beating again.

"Give me 400 volts," the doctor said. "Clear," he spoke as he applied the leads to Xavier's chest. His body jumped up and then back down on the bed. The monitor continued to show a flat line.

"Eight hundred volts," he instructed. "Clear," he again placed the leads on Xavier's chest. His body flopped.

"Goddammit," Blaze said. He figured it would be easy to fight a self-defense charge, but it would be a whole new ballgame if Xavier died. He would be facing murder or manslaughter charges.

Xavier's heart monitor was still showing a flat line.

"Dear God, please let this son of a bitch make it," Blaze prayed.

"Seventeen hundred volts," the doctor yelled. Blaze knew from watching reruns of one of his favorite shows *ER* that this was the highest voltage that could be safely administered. It was all or nothing. "Clear," the doctor yelled one final time.

Everything seemed to move in slow motion. Keya raised her head up from Khalil's chest. She peered into the room. Xavier's body jerked and flinched. All eyes turned to the heart monitor. "Beep, beep, beep," could be heard sounding off. The entire room breathed a sigh of relief.

Keya grabbed Khalil. "Oh my God. He's ok."

Blaze turned to leave before she had a chance to see him watching.

Xavier had cheated death once again.

Keya squeezed. Khalil didn't mind. She held on to him until the doctors began exiting the room.

"Can I see him?" Keya asked.

"Only for a second," the doctor responded. "We are moving him to the intensive care unit so that he can be watched around the clock."

Keya started towards the door. When she realized Khalil wasn't moving with her, she turned to him. "Come with me."

Khalil paused. "Sure."

Keya spoke to Xavier. "Hey dude. Stop scaring me." Keya hoped that he could hear her. "I love you X."

"Ok ma'am, we have to get him moved," a hospital orderly spoke.

Keya stepped back. The orderly unlocked the wheels on the bed and began pushing it out of the door. Keya knew it would be at least an hour before she would get a chance to see Xavier again. He would need to be checked in and have his vitals taken by the ICU nurses.

"Thank you," Keya told Khalil. "I really appreciate you staying with me through all of this. You could have just as easily bailed on me. She reached up to give him a hug. Khalil was just as handsome as Blaze was, although their features were very different. Khalil had a tad bit stronger looking build. While Blaze was sexy chocolate, Khalil's skin tone was a mixture between caramel and cocoa. Khalil stood a good four inches taller than Blaze, and his dimpled smile could melt any girl's heart. That's exactly what Khalil was doing, melting Keya's heart. When she released him, she only stepped back an inch. Their bodies were still touching. Khalil stared into her eyes. When he lowered his head, she met his lips half way as they softly pecked. Khalil used his tongue to trace her lips. Keya loved the feeling of his mouth on her. She leaned into the kiss, tasting his tongue and pulling it into her mouth. Khalil allowed his hands to roam her body.

He had wanted to grab her ass from the moment he saw how plump it was. He squeezed. Using both his hands to cup her ass, he lifted her off the ground. Keya wrapped her legs around his waist. Khalil walked over and pressed her body against the wall. He moved his lips to her neck. He kissed and licked his way down to her breasts. He allowed her body to slide down his, as she reconnected her feet with the floor. Keya's breathing intensified. It had been ages since a man touched her body in this way. Khalil unbuttoned her shirt. He took her bra and pulled it up over her breasts.

"Beautiful," he spoke as they bounced from being set free. Khalil used both his hands to cover both of her breasts at the same time. He took her nipples between his thumb and forefinger. Gently, he applied pressure. Small moans departed Keya's lips. She needed this. Her body needed this. She felt her pussy jumping like pop rocks used to jump in her mouth when she was a little girl. By the time Khalil slid his tongue across her nipple, Keya was climaxing. She had an orgasm so fast that Khalil laughed. Keya smiled.

"Guess it's been a while," Khalil said.

"Longer than you can imagine," Keya replied. She refused to tell him that she was still a virgin.

CHAPTER FOURTEEN
BLAZE

Blaze said a silent prayer on his way back to BJ's room. "Lord, thank you for letting that fool live." It wasn't the best prayer, but it didn't need to be. He was simply thanking God for making things work in his favor.

Blaze was about to walk back into the room when he remembered that Khalil had told him to call Mackie. He pulled his phone from his pocket and dialed Mackie's number. The phone rang several times before her voicemail picked. Blaze disconnected the call without leaving a message. He dialed Diesel's number.

"What's up Blaze?" Diesel answered the call.

"Not much. What's going on over there?" Blaze asked.

"Nothing, I'm on my way back to the house. Mackie wanted a baked potato from H&J's."

Blaze wanted to blast him but he didn't because he knew how persuasive Mackie could be. And with Diesel feeling her like he was, she could probably get him to do anything that she wanted. "How long have you been gone?"

"About thirty or forty minutes. Is everything ok?" Diesel started to worry.

"I'm not sure. Khalil told me to check on her but I haven't had a chance to ask him what was going on. I just tried to call her but she didn't answer the phone." Diesel got nervous.

"Ok, I'm about fifteen minutes out. I'll call you or have her to call you when I get there. Maybe she was just in the bathroom or something."

Blaze walked into BJ's room. He was asleep. Khalil's son was asleep in the bed with him. Blaze was grateful that he had such a great support system for his son. Being in the game, it was hard to trust people. When good people came along you had to try to hold on to them for as long as you could.

"Hey baby, did you find Khalil?" Ms. Hamilton asked.

"Yes ma'am. He's helping a friend. He said he would be back shortly," Blaze told her.

"Ok, well you go ahead and get on out of here. I've got this covered."

"Thank you Ms. Hamilton."

"Will you tell Khalil to call me when he gets back?" Blaze asked her.

"I sure will."

Blaze hugged her before slipping her an envelope with money in it. "Now you know I don't need your money. I swear, between you and Khalil, I am going to be a millionaire. Seeing after these boys gives an old lady like me something to do before dying," she laughed.

Blaze kissed her on the cheek and walked from the room. He hated to hear her talk about dying. She was the only grandmother figure that BJ had ever known. If something ever happened to her, he, Mackie and BJ would be at a loss, not to mention Khalil and his son.

Blaze had a funky feeling about not being able to get in touch with Mackie. He knew how strong-willed Mackie was. Blaze decided to drive by to check on her himself before going to see Aleah.

As soon as Blaze pulled onto the main street, his phone began ringing. Khalil's name flashed across his screen. "What's up Kha?"

"Dude, Mackie was up in Xavier's room."

"What?" Blaze was pissed. "I told her ass to stay put."

"Yeah I know. Where the hell is Diesel's ass?" Khalil asked.

"I just got off the phone with him. He said Mackie sent him to pick up some food in Oak Cliff."

"I swear he don't need to be Mackie's fucking handler." Khalil was just as pissed as Blaze. "That fool is so fucking sprung by her, he'd probably let her walk into the damn police station and blow the muthafucka up if she batted her damn eyes at him."

"What the hell do you mean sprung," Blaze asked. "Are you saying that he's slept with my sister?"

"Naw man, that's just a figure of speech," Khalil explained. "Even if I knew something like that I wouldn't tell yo' ignorant ass."

Blaze had to laugh. Everybody knew how protective he was of Mackie. He knew that Mackie was fucking, he just didn't want to hear about it or know any of the dudes that she had been with.

"So when Keya walked in and saw Mackie, she was pissed. She started popping off at the mouth. Before I had a chance to get Mackie, she knocked the shit out of Keya. I'm guessing Xavier could hear what was going on because the machines starting sounding off. I made Mackie leave. The doctors came in and put us out of the room. That's when you saw us in the hallway."

"Shit," Blaze cursed.

"Keya was talking about calling the police and having Mackie arrested. I think I might have calmed her down, but I'm still not sure if she is going to file charges or not," Khalil told him.

"Alright man," Blaze responded. "Good looking out."

Blaze disconnected the phone and yelled. He was sick of Mackie's disobedient ass.

Blaze picked his phone back up. He dialed Aleah's number and she answered on the second ring. Just hearing her say hello had put a smile on his face.

"I miss you beautiful," Blaze crooned.

Aleah laughed, "I miss you too. Are you on your way home?"

"Not just yet. I have something that just popped up that I need to take care of."

Aleah got quiet. She wanted to ask but was afraid of what the answer might be. Had one of his workers messed up and he was going to handle them, or was a shipment of drugs coming in that he needed to go pick up. All these thoughts ran through her mind.

Blaze sensed her uneasiness. "I need to swing by the house to check on Mackie; she didn't answer the phone when I called. And Diesel left to go pick up food. So I just want to check on her," he explained.

Aleah breathed out in relief. She was happy that he took good care of his sister. Mackie was lucky to have him.

"Ok," she answered.

"Do you want me to pick up something for us to eat?" he asked.

"No," she smiled. "I cooked. I hope you don't mind."

"Of course not. I can't remember the last time I've had a home cooked meal," Blaze said.

"Ok, hurry home and be safe," Aleah told him.

Blaze felt it. He was falling for her. He wondered how she felt about him. More importantly, how she felt about her husband.

"Aleah," Blaze called her name before she hung up the phone.

"Yes," she answered.

"There was an incident at the hospital with Xavier today. He's stable now, but you might want to check on him," Blaze told her.

Aleah was quiet. Blaze waited for her response.

She finally answered. "Thanks for telling me that Blaze. I appreciate it."

"You're welcome."

"Hurry home," she told him once again.

"You're not going to the hospital?" he asked.

"No, I'm not. I don't want anything bad to happen to Xavier, but what we had is over. I'll pray for him and Keya, but that part of my life is over."

Blaze was happy to hear those words.

"See you soon," he spoke.

"Ok," Aleah answered.

CHAPTER FIFTEEN
ALEAH

Aleah sat on the sofa thinking about what Blaze had told her. She had been thinking all morning. Being in a new environment seemed to allow her to really think about her situation and focus on herself for a change. Her entire adulthood had been consumed with taking care of Xavier and Keya, neither of whom needed nor wanted her around anymore. If she were honest with herself, they hadn't needed her in a long time. They were each holding on to something that should have never been.

"I'm still young. I still have a whole lot of life left in me," Aleah spoke. She hoped that Xavier survived and got his life together. She hoped that Keya would find her a nice man to settle down with. She was too young to be so intertwined in Xavier's life. She knew why they were so close. They only had each other, but it wasn't healthy for her. She needed to live her own life.

Aleah thought about Xavier and Mackie. She wondered how Mackie felt about Xavier. She was so distraught after she shot him. It seemed as though she really cared for him. She didn't know Mackie well at all, but she didn't want her to be subjected to Xavier's abusive personality. Blaze would surely kill Xavier if he laid a hand on Mackie. It just wouldn't be good for anybody involved if they got together permanently. "But who I am I tell anybody about who to get involved with. I've let this man practically ruin my life. But not anymore," she said. "That part of my life is over. This is the new and improved Aleah." She planned to ask Blaze if she could stay at his house until she could figure how she was going to manage things. Everything she had was in Xavier's name. She didn't even have access to their bank account. If she needed money, Xavier would give her cash or a gift card. She had no clue what they had in savings. *I really don't give a shit what he has*, Aleah thought. *My freedom and my dignity is all that I need. Surely I can get a job somewhere. I have a freaking degree.* "But I've never had a job. I have no work history. Who's going to hire me without an ounce of experience? Guess I'll cross that bridge when I get to it," Aleah voiced.

Aleah picked up her phone as it began ringing. She thought it might be Blaze calling back. She looked at the screen and Keya's name popped up. Aleah debated on answering it.

"Hello," she finally pressed the talk button.

"Hey Aleah."

"Hey," Aleah responded back.

"I just wanted to let you know that they moved Xavier to ICU. He flat lined a little while ago, but they were able to revive him," Keya told her.

Aleah paused before asking if he was stable.

"Yes, they moved him so that he could be monitored more closely."

"Oh," Aleah replied.

"Well, I just wanted you to know.

"Ok."

"Ok," Keya repeated.

"Thanks for letting me know," Aleah said. As much as she wanted to, she couldn't be mean to Keya.

"Bye," Keya ended the call.

Aleah was ready to put Xavier and Keya out of her mind. She wanted to prepare for Blaze. The food was ready. Now it was time to get herself together. She hoped Mackie wouldn't mind. She went into Mackie's room to look for something sexy to wear for Blaze.

She loved how Mackie had her room decorated. She used rich bold colors. "Probably to match her personality," Aleah stated. Everyone within ten feet of Mackie could tell she wasn't a shy person and she oozed self-confidence. Aleah thought of how different their personalities must be. She wondered if that had been the attraction for Xavier to her.

"Whatever," she said walking over to the armoire and pulled it open. She slid the top drawer out. It looked like mostly panties and bras. Aleah was hoping to find some lingerie that Mackie hadn't worn yet. The second drawer that she opened contained just what she needed. It was like it had been sitting there waiting on her. The tags were still attached. "Yes," Aleah cheered. She was determined to look so good that Blaze had no choice but to make love to her tonight.

Aleah was about to push the drawer back in when she noticed the edges of a book sticking out. She pulled it from underneath the clothes. She didn't think people still wrote in diaries, but here was Mackie's with the words *My Diary* written across the front. Aleah debated on opening the book. She knew it was wrong to invade someone's privacy this way, but it could answer a whole lot of questions that she had about her and Xavier and when they'd actually started seeing each other.

"I can't," Aleah stated and shoved the book back in its place. She turned out the light and closed the door to Mackie's room. Things were falling into place for a perfect evening.

CHAPTER SIXTEEN
MACKIE

When Mackie pulled back up to the house, Diesel's car was already back in the driveway. "Damn," she said. "Fucking around with Keya's ass made me spend more time than I had planned at the hospital. I was supposed to be in and out. I just needed to see Xavier."

She hoped Diesel hadn't called Blaze looking for her. If he did, she knew that meant that Blaze would be on his way.

Mackie jumped out of the car and ran to the door. She pushed it open, walked through and closed it quickly. When she looked to the left, Diesel sat in chair in the living area looking pissed.

"Hey," Mackie said weakly.

Diesel didn't say a word. He was beyond pissed.

"Diesel," Mackie said.

"Shut up Mackie. If all you're going to do is lie, save it."

Mackie heard a car door close. She looked out the front window and saw Blaze getting out of the car. "You fucking called Blaze on me!"

"I didn't call Blaze. Khalil told him that he saw you at the hospital. If you would have answered my damn call instead of sending it to voicemail, you would have known that.

Blaze walked through door looking just as pissed off as Diesel had been looking.

"Mackie, what hell is wrong with you?" Blaze roared. "Didn't I tell you to stay away from the goddamned hospital? I am trying to keep you protected but you are making shit too damn hard. What if Keya calls the police on you? Huh? Your ass could be locked up for assault."

"You didn't hear what she said to me," Mackie said.

"No I didn't. But it's irrelevant because your ass wasn't supposed to be there," Blaze shouted.

"Blaze calm down," Diesel said.

"Calm down? Nigga, you need to calm the fuck up. Hell, you were supposed to be watching her and keeping her out of trouble. But naw, your ass is running around here like a damn servant," Blaze continued ranting.

"Don't yell at him," Mackie defended.

"Don't do what?" Blaze had that 'I got shit on my shoes' look on his face. "Oh so y'all gone tag team me, huh?"

"No, it's not like that," Diesel spoke.

"Well how the fuck is it Diesel? Tell me how is it that you were supposed to be watching her but she ends up at the exact place that I told her not to come?" Blaze was on a roll.

"Blaze, stop it," Mackie interrupted. "I'm not a kid."

"Really Mackie, because you just did some kid like shit," Blaze told her.

Mackie screamed and ran from the room. She slammed her door with extra effect. She wanted Blaze to feel her level of anger.

Blaze turned back to Diesel. "Whatever it is that you are feeling for Mackie, you better ball that shit up and put in your fucking pocket. I love that ignorant ass girl in there," he pointed towards the room. "And I will fuck you up if something happens to her."

Diesel felt like shit. He had allowed his feelings for Mackie to cloud his judgment. Blaze was right. He knew he shouldn't have left Mackie at the house by herself. He should have just ordered something to be delivered or cooked what was in the refrigerator.

"Diesel," Blaze called his name. "Diesel," he had to say a second time. He knew that Diesel felt bad, but he needed him focused on the job at hand, and that was keeping Mackie out of the spotlight. Diesel looked up. "Can you set aside your feelings and do what Mackie needs and not what she wants?"

"Yeah man," Diesel answered.

"Alright, I'll be at Frost Farms tonight if you need anything," Blaze told him.

"I'm out Mackie," Blaze yelled. He knew she wouldn't answer. She was stubborn and hated being criticized in any form. She could go days without talking to Blaze, but if he knew he was right, he didn't care. She would eventually start talking back to him in few days.

Blaze dapped Diesel up. He actually liked the idea of Mackie with Diesel, but all that needed to be tabled right now.

Mackie had been listening with her ear pressed against the door. Diesel hadn't denied his feelings for her when Blaze brought it up. *He really does have feelings for me*, she thought. Mackie had never given Diesel any thought as far as a relationship. He was her boy. She was his girl. They had that Bonnie and Clyde thing going without the hassle of lust, love and sex.

Mackie opened her door and walked back into the living area. Diesel was still sitting in the same seat that he had been when she ran from the room. He looked up when he heard her walk into the room.

"I'm sorry," she apologized.

Diesel didn't respond. He didn't believe her. Mackie was never sorry about anything that she did. He knew her better than she knew herself. He knew that she had been listening at the door when Blaze was talking. He knew that she now knew that he wanted her. But he was going to do exactly as Blaze had suggested. The feelings that he had for her would be put away. He had a job to do.

"Can I trust you to not leave the house without me?" Diesel asked.

"Yes," Mackie told him.

"Good. I'm going to bed. I'll see you in the morning." Diesel had no intention of going to sleep right now, but he didn't want to talk to Mackie. "Your food is in the kitchen." He stretched out on the couch and closed his eyes.

"Did you hear me apologize?" Mackie snapped.

Diesel ignored her again.

"Whatever," Mackie stormed from the room. Diesel opened his eyes when he heard her in the kitchen. It sounded like she was trying to wake up the dead. She slammed drawers, the refrigerator and microwave doors.

Mackie walked back into the room. "I just wanted to see if he was okay."

"I get it Mackie, you care about him," Diesel shouted. He got up off of the couch and walked to the backdoor. He opened it and went out to sit on the patio.

Mackie stood there with her mouth hanging open. *He's jealous*, she thought.

CHAPTER SEVENTEEN
KEYA

Keya sat in the intensive care unit waiting room smiling. Khalil had asked for her phone number and he had given her his. *He wants to see me again, he'd said. He seems like a really nice guy.*

Keya's smile turned to a frown when she touched the side of her face. Her face still hurt from Mackie hitting her. She definitely had payback coming. "I'm not letting that bitch get away with this shit," Keya said.

"What bitch get away with what?" her nurse friend walked up and heard her last comment.

"Hey Damien," Keya smiled. She hadn't seen him since the night that he told her who Blaze and Mackie really were.

"Hey Chica," Damien hugged her.

"I guess you heard what happened with Xavier?" Keya asked.

"Yes girlfriend, you know that's all everybody is talking about around here."

"What are they saying?" Keya wanted to know.

"That y'all had some straight up fatal attraction shit going on," Damien said.

Keya laughed. "People never get shit right and always want to spread the untruth."

"So what happened?" Damien persisted.

"Apparently, Xavier has been dating Mackie," Keya told him.

"Mack Bitch?" Damien was shocked.

"Unfortunately," Mackie said.

"Girl, is that why you were pumping for information about the Carter's?"

"Yeah, I wasn't sure. I had only seen Xavier talking to her. I didn't know that they were actually in a relationship. If I had known, I would have shut that shit down real quick. I knew some bullshit like this could jump off," Keya explained.

"So what's your sister-in-law saying about all of this? She must be crushed to know that Xavier was messing around," Damien said.

"Damien, don't stand there and bullshit with me. You know damn well you already heard about her and Blaze."

Damien laughed. "But girl, those are just rumors. I need to hear it firsthand."

"I swear you are too much. I guess my family has been really busy lately and I was none the wiser," Keya told him.

"Well damn, that's some Jerry Springer shit right there," Damien said. "So Blaze shot Xavier?"

"Yeah, from what I'm hearing, Xavier followed Aleah to Blaze's house. Some kind of fight broke out and Blaze shot him."

"Wow, that's strange."

"Why?" Aleah asked.

"Because Blaze usually doesn't shoot anybody. He hates using guns. He usually just kills a nigga with his bare hands," Damien said.

Keya had forgotten that Damien's boyfriend used to work for the Carter's before he was killed.

"That's the second time that I've heard that," Keya stated.

"Really, who told you that?"

"A friend of mine, Khalil," Keya said.

"Khalil Hamilton?"

"Actually, I don't know his last name. I just met him today," Keya explained.

"Where did you meet him?"

"Here at the hospital," Keya answered.

"Was he with Blaze?"

"Yes, he was."

"Khalil Hamilton," Damien repeated.

"Do you know him?"

"Everybody does, except you," Damien told her. "He's heavy in the game. Blaze's right-hand man."

Keya sighed.

"Why, was he trying to get with you?" Damien asked.

"I don't know," Keya lied.

She felt like she could really connect with Khalil, but she didn't want to be a part of that lifestyle. *Is every damn body heavy in the game?* she wondered. *Why can't I meet a nice guy that's legit?*

"Well girl, let me get back to work before they come looking for me," Damien laughed. "You let me know if you need anything. And remember, all things work out for the good for those who believe."

Keya smiled. She loved that scripture. Damien had misquoted it, but the meaning was still the same.

Keya needed to make a decision quick; she was trying to decide if she was going to press charges against Mackie for hitting her. Keya knew that she was talking a lot of shit, but that still doesn't give anybody the right to resort to violence.

As Keya sat there thinking, her thoughts went to Aleah. She hadn't seen or heard from her all day. Keya didn't blame her for not showing up. The two times that she did come, they had argued and fought. Honestly, Xavier was just as much at fault for all of this, as Blaze and Aleah were. He's been cheating with Mackie. They are all adults and making adult decisions with adult consequences.

Keya decided to call Aleah. She wondered if she would answer this time. The phone rang several times. Keya was just about to hang up when she heard Aleah say hello. The conversation was awkward. Keya just told her about Xavier's condition and then ended the call. *It wasn't much but it was a start,* Keya thought.

"Hey, I found you."

Keya turned towards the entrance to the waiting room. Khalil stood there holding two cups of coffee and smiling.

"This is the third waiting room that I've been to. Do you know how many intensive care units this hospital has?" he asked.

Keya smiled. "I do. I work here."

"Really, what do you do?" Khalil asked.

"I'm a nurse," Keya answered.

"So that's how everyone knew your name. And here I thought you were just really friendly and nice, and that everybody wanted to get to know you just like I do," Khalil explained.

Keya blushed.

"I brought you coffee. I was trying to decide between coffee and soda. Coffee won the battle. I remembered that you didn't get a chance to drink your coffee earlier.

"Thank you," Keya reached for the cup.

"Do you mind if I join you?" Khalil asked.

"No, I don't mind."

"So have you had a chance to see your brother?"

"Just for a little while. I have to wait for the next visiting hours to go back again," Keya told him.

There was an awkward pause. Keya wanted to ask him about what Damien said. She wanted to know about his connection to Blaze, but she didn't know how to bring it up. She wanted to know if he was really interested in her or just trying to get information for Blaze and Mackie.

"Look," Keya started. "I've heard a lot of rumors and I need to know from you before we move forward what it is that you want from me. I don't like playing games. If it's information that you're trying to get from me just ask. If it's just a piece of ass that you are after, just tell me that too."

Khalil loved her feisty attitude. He smiled.

"I'm a big girl. I can handle the truth."

Khalil shut her up by leaning over and covering her mouth with his. Khalil winced as she dropped her cup of coffee on him for the second time that day.

"I'm sorry," Keya jumped up to grab napkins from the counter. She began wiping the coffee off of Khalil's arms. She wiped down his shirt and without realizing, wiped down his crotch. When she felt Khalil's dick growing hard, she jumped and pulled her hand back. "I'm sorry," she said again.

"It's ok," Khalil told.

"You probably think I'm a klutz."

"No, I don't think that. I think you are a beautiful, sexy woman," Khalil complimented.

Keya didn't know what to say.

Khalil leaned in close to her. "I love your lips. They're sexy as hell."

Keya's kitty started jumping again. She was lost. This was all new to her. Again, she didn't know what to say.

Khalil kissed her ever so softly. He held her head in his hands. Their tongues danced around together before they were interrupted by the detective walking into the waiting room.

He cleared his throat to get their attention. "Ms. Thomas."

"Hi detective," Keya spoke.

"Hello." The detective turned to look at Khalil. "I don't think we have met." He extended his hand.

Khalil looked at his hand like he had shit on it. "I don't think we have," Khalil responded, not offering him his name. He stepped away from Keya and the detective.

"What's his problem?" the detective asked Keya.

"Just a little stressed," Keya lied. "What's going on?"

"I heard there was a little altercation here earlier involving you and Mackie Carter," he stated. "Isn't she the sister of the man who shot your brother?"

"Who said that?" Keya asked.

"Oh, we hear everything," the detective smiled. He turned to look at Khalil when he said it.

Khalil was listening. He hated this detective. He was an asshole. Khalil had met him on more than one occasion. He didn't know what his motive was for saying that they had never met before. Khalil tried to avoid him any time their paths crossed. He had made Khalil propositions for information on Blaze and Mackie over the past few months. He was as shady as they came. It didn't surprise him that he was here now pumping Keya for information. He was pissed that he couldn't get anything on Blaze and Mackie. They ran a tight ship and couldn't be linked to anything. But this shit that's going on right now had the potential of wrecking the entire setup.

"So Mackie Carter assaulted you," the detective asked.

"Um," Keya looked at Khalil. She knew she had said earlier that she was going to call the police and press charges, but now that the detective was front and center and asking questions, she didn't know how far she wanted to take it.

"I wouldn't call it an assault," Keya replied.

The detective looked pissed for half a second but quickly recovered. Khalil smirked.

"If someone puts their hands on you without your permission, that's an assault," the detective stated.

"I know what an assault is, detective. And If I ever feel that I have been assaulted, I will let you know," Keya told him.

"So your team Carter now?" he asked. "I wonder what your brother would have to say if he wakes up from his coma." The detective was clearly trying to get under her skin.

"I am team Keya," she replied.

"We do have witnesses and we plan to charge Mackie Carter with assault, with or without your cooperation. Just know that you'll be called and sworn in as a witness," the detective informed.

"Why are you here?" Keya asked the detective.

Khalil loved it. She was standing her ground.

"So Khalil, do you know where Mackie is?"

"Oh, so now you know my name?" Khalil responded.

"Yeah, you look more familiar now that I've gotten a closer look. So where is your boss?"

"I'm my own boss," Khalil stated.

"Yeah. If you see Mackie, tell her not to leave town. I need to talk to her," the detective requested.

Once the detective left the room, Keya asked Khalil if he was ok.

"Yeah, he's just a prick," Khalil stated.

"So you do know him?" Keya asked.

"Unfortunately. He's a certified asshole. Thanks for not feeding into his bullshit," Khalil told her. "I have some things that I need to take care of, but I really would love to see you later today, if you're not busy."

"I'd like that, but I don't want to be gone too long or go too far in case something happens with Xavier."

"Ok, seven o'clock good? We can just go around the corner to a little restaurant on Live Oak," Khalil told her.

"Sounds good," Keya responded.

Khalil kissed her one more time before leaving.

I don't know what the hell I am getting into, but it sure feels good to me. I'll just sort the rest of it out later, Keya thought to herself.

CHAPTER EIGHTEEN
BLAZE

Blaze was still pissed at Mackie, but excited to finally be heading home to see Aleah. He so looked forward to the day that he could leave all this bullshit behind and start over in a new city on the other side of the country. He'd decided that to make things a little easier for Mackie when they moved that he would even let her pick the city. They could even move to another country if she wanted to. Just as long as they got the hell out of Dallas.

Blaze dialed Aleah's number. "Hey sweetheart. I'm finally on my way."

"Yay," Aleah cheered. "I've been waiting for you all day."

"I love the sound of that," Blaze said.

"I hope you have your energy up because I'm ready to rock your world Mr. Carter."

Blaze smiled. "Have you been drinking?" It sounded like Aleah was slurring her words just a bit.

Aleah laughed. "Just a little bit. I got bored waiting for you."

"Well at least you're at the house and won't need to drive anywhere," Blaze teased.

"I see you're not going to let me live that nightmare down."

"Nope, never," Blaze laughed. "Shit," Blaze stated.

"What's wrong?" Aleah asked.

"I'm being pulled over by the police." At least that's what he assumed. It was an unmarked car with one of those lights thrown on the top to the side. "Let me call you back."

"Ok, be safe," Aleah told him. She was worried not only because of his lifestyle, but also because of all the killing that was taking place around the country of young black men. Aleah had prayed for all the families of those young men who had been senselessly murdered.

Blaze pulled the car over. He knew this was some more bullshit. He never drove over the speed limit; as a matter a fact, he always drove five miles under the speed limit. His car was always in tip top shape; no broken tail lights, and registration and inspection stickers up-to-date. "Yea, straight bullshit," Blaze said when he looked and saw who had pulled him over. It was the two agents that had interviewed him yesterday.

"Slowly out, your hands out of the window," Agent Blanton stated with his gun drawn. Agent Zamora was on the other side of the car, looking bored shitless.

Blaze put his hands out the window as instructed.

Agent Blanton reached down an opened the door. "Step out of the car sir."

Blaze continued to follow his instructions.

"Turn around," Blanton said.

When Blaze turned around, he put the cuffs on him.

"What's this all about," Blaze asked.

"I'm asking the questions," he barked at Blaze.

"Hey Blaze," Zamora spoke.

Blaze threw his head up acknowledging her.

"We need to search your car. There was a bank robbery about a mile from here. Your car matches the description of the getaway vehicle," Blanton stated.

Blaze sighed. He didn't have time to play games with these two.

"Search the car Zamora."

"Why do I have to search the car?" Zamora asked.

"Geez, well watch the perp, I'll search the car. If he runs, shoot him," Blanton laughed at his attempt to be funny.

Blanton started looking through Blaze's car. He was being a true asshole, tossing all of Blaze's things around in the car. Blaze played it cool. He could replace anything in there that Blanton fucked up. He knew Blanton was trying to get him to relax.

Blaze turned his attention to Zamora. He knew she was feeling him. He decided to take advantage of it. He could always use her as inside connection. When he turned to look at her, she was already looking at him and licking her lips.

"Don't you need to search me and read me my rights?" Blaze whispered.

Her smile got even bigger.

She walked towards Blaze with a little extra sway in her hips.

Zamora slowly walked around Blaze. She stopped, standing directly behind him. She slid one foot between his, bumping each. "Spread your legs."

Blaze did as instructed. She leaned in, pressing her breasts again his back.

"You have the right to remain silent," she whispered.

She took her hands and placed them on his shoulders.

"Anything you say may be used against you in court."

She slid her hands down his arms. Both hands moved around his body landing on his chest.

"You have the right to the presence of an attorney before and during any questioning."

She moved her hands down slowly sliding them into his pockets.

"If you cannot afford an attorney, one will be appointed for you free of charge before any questioning if you want."

She took her left hand and went further over until she felt his dick. "Do you wish to waive these rights?"

She squeezed. "Nice size," she whispered.

"Zamora, what are you doing?" Blanton asked as he rose up from the car.

"I'm searching his person to make sure he doesn't have anything on him," she answered while still clutching Blaze's dick.

That caused Blaze to become rock hard. Blanton didn't have a clue what she had in hand stuffed in his pocket.

"He's clean?" Blanton asked.

"Yes he is," Zamora responded.

"Oh, I forgot to check the trunk," Blanton said as he pushed the button from inside the car to open it. He walked to the back of the car and again, started tossing things around. Zamora move in front of Blaze and used her key to un-cuff him. As soon as she did, Blaze grabbed her pussy and squeezed. He used his free had to do the same thing to her breasts. She let out a slight moan. "When are you going to let me taste it?" he asked.

"Soon," she responded.

"There's nothing back her either," Blanton said.

Blaze released the grip that he had on her private parts just before Blanton walked up behind his partner.

"What color was the car that the bank robbers were driving?" Blaze asked.

"White," Blanton laughed.

Blaze didn't say another word. He walked to his car, got in, and pulled off. His car was black.

He picked up his phone and called Aleah back.

"I'm on my way."

"Thank God," Aleah breathed.

CHAPTER NINETEEN
ALEAH

Aleah was glad to hear back from Blaze. She was worried sick until he called back. She changed into the lingerie that she swiped from Mackie's room. She loved the color against her skin tone. There was very little left to the imagination. It had a Fredrick's of Hollywood label in the piece. Aleah loved their lingerie. It was much sexier than the lingerie that Victoria's Secret sold. Victoria's secret focused more on push-ups. Pushing her breasts up were the least of her problems. She needed more help in the ass the department. *This open cup naughty bra is going to make Blaze lose his mind,* she thought. The matching bottoms were a pair of cut out naughty nickers. *Just what I need to make my ass look bigger.*

Aleah set up the music and moved her chair into view of the front door. She'd selected Beyoncé's "Partition". She had been naughty dancing to this song since it came out. She never got a chance to dance to it for Xavier, but tonight she wanted to share it with Blaze. She had perfected each of the moves that Beyoncé did in the video. The only thing that she wished she had was a pole.

When Aleah heard Blaze's car pull into the driveway, she downed the rest of her wine, turned down the lights, rushed to the chair, opened her legs and draped them over each arm of the chair. As the door knob turned, she pushed the button to allow Beyoncé's voice to flow throughout the room.

Aleah's pussy was the first thing that Blaze saw when he walked through the door. It was all it took for his already aroused dick to get even harder.

Driver roll up the partition please
Driver roll up the partition please
I don't need you seeing 'yonce on her knees
Took 45 minutes to get all dressed up
We ain't even gonna make it to this club
Now my mascara running, red lipstick smudged
Oh he so horny, he want to fuck
He bucked all my buttons, he ripped my blouse
He Monica Lewinski all on my gown

Aleah's body was moving in ways that made Blaze want to end her show right now. Just like Beyoncé's words said, he was horny and wanted to fuck.

Oh there daddy, d-daddy didn't bring the towel
Oh baby, b-baby we slow it down
Took 45 minutes to get all dressed up
We ain't even gonna make it to this club

Take all of me
I just wanna be the girl you like, girl you like
The kind of girl you like, girl you like
Take all of me
I just wanna be the girl you like, girl you like
The kinda girl you like
Is right here with me

That was it. Blaze couldn't wait another second. He made his way over to Aleah. She hadn't seen him. She was dancing with her eyes closed. When she bumped into him she jumped and opened her eyes. "You're supposed to be over there," Aleah pointed.

"No, I'm supposed to be over here doing this." Blaze reached out and grabbed her ass, pulling her to him. He kissed her rough and hard. Aleah followed his lead. They were intense and greedy in trying to please each other and themselves. Aleah began undressing him. It was like they were both starving for sex. Blaze sucked and licked on her neck as she practically tore his clothes from his body. Blaze sat her back down in the chair and placed her legs back in the position they were in when he walked through the door. He had full access to her sweet spot. He lowered his head and plunged his tongue in and out. He was relentless as he used his tongue to touch every part of her pussy that it could reach. Aleah climaxed several times. Blaze licked up her juices like it was the sweetest thing he had ever tasted. Each time she exploded in his mouth, she thought he was done. But he continued sucking between her folds like his life depended on it. Aleah couldn't believe the sensations coursing throughout her veins. He had truly taken her to another planet. She had no doubt that he could eat her pussy all day long and she would enjoy every minute of it.

Aleah was weak, but she wasn't going to let him get away without her working her magic on him. She reached down, pulling him up to her. She kissed him, tasting all her juices on his lips. She switched places with him and stroked his dick long and hard before sliding her lips down on it. Blaze was huge. But Aleah had mastered the art of sucking dick a long time ago. Every *Redbook* and *Cosmopolitan* magazine article with blowjob in the title, she had read. Aleah kept her eyes fixated on Blaze's eyes. She could tell that he was amazed as she continued taking him into her mouth inch by inch.

Aleah was proud of her deep throat. She'd learned that the meatus is supersensitive. That's where she chose to start. She used her tongue to first circle then apply pressure to that little hole on the tip of his penis. Blaze rewarded her with gut wrenching moan. He grabbed her head and held it in place. She knew that meant he wanted her to stay right there in that spot. She obliged. She worked that spot for some time before she started moving her mouth up and down his shaft. Blaze was in heaven. As he started moving towards cumming, Aleah took him deeper into her mouth and this time allowed her lips and tongue to make contact with his balls. Within seconds, Blaze was exploding in her mouth. Aleah loved it. She sucked as hard as she could, pulling every drop of semen that she could from his body.

"Oh my God," Blaze breathed. "That was the best."

"I couldn't let you outdo me," Aleah responded.

CHAPTER TWENTY
MACKIE

Mackie stood looking out the backdoor at Diesel sitting on the patio. For the first time in a long time, she was at a loss. She didn't know what to do. Her feelings were all mixed up. She'd never really even given Diesel much thought. He was her best friend.

Could she date her best friend? What about Xavier? *I was thinking he was the one, maybe not,* Mackie pondered.

Mackie sat on the couch. She still had a direct view of Diesel. She picked up her cell phone and headphones. She turned on her playlist. Rick James and Tina Marie filled her ears with "Fire and Desire". Mackie snapped her head to look at her phone. She couldn't believe the song that was playing. She and Diesel had sung this song together at the talent show their freshman year in high school. They'd auditioned for the talent show as a joke, but when they posted the list of performers and their names were on it, they got serious about it. They had kissed on the stage but it was just a part of the show. After that, everyone thought that they were a couple. Diesel's girlfriend broke up with him. He didn't have any more girlfriends for the rest of high school. Not that he couldn't, because girls were always trying to get with him.

Mackie wondered if this was a sign. She listened to words and watched Diesel, wondering if he had felt anything for her back when they were in high school, or if he had developed feelings for her after they'd become adults.

Mackie wondered how long he was going to stay out on the patio. The slow jams from her playlists continued to make her think about the possibility of a relationship with Diesel. Mackie was scared. If they dated and it didn't work out, where would that leave them? Mackie stretched out on the couch, keeping her eyes glued to Diesel. The longer she watched him, the heavier her eyes became. Eventually they closed all together.

By the time Diesel came back into the house, Mackie was fast asleep. He stood and watched her sleep. *She's beautiful*, he thought. Diesel felt silly. He was making a fool of himself. *She's never going to want you*, he told himself. Diesel began turning lights off. He walked over to Mackie and took her headphones off. She stirred a bit but didn't wake up.

Diesel reached down scooping her into his arms. He walked towards the bedroom as Mackie snuggled into his chest. He gently placed her on the bed and reached back to pull the blanket up over her. As he was tucking her in, Mackie's eyes opened. Their eyes met. Mackie touched his hand. She reached up grabbing his shirt. She pulled him towards her.

"Mackie what are you doing?"

She didn't answer. She kissed his lips.

"Mackie no," Diesel tried to say. Mackie ignored him. "We can't," Diesel said. Diesel continued trying to pull away, but Mackie had a strong grip on his shirt.

"You know you want me," Mackie stated. "Tell me you want me."

Diesel didn't say anything.

"Please, I need to hear it Diesel. Tell me you want me."

Diesel relented. "I want you." He leaned into the kiss. "I want you so bad. I've always wanted you," Diesel told her.

"What about Shay?" Mackie asked.

"She's not you," Diesel answered.

"What about Blaze? He's going to kill me."

"I can handle Blaze," Mackie whispered.

"What about Xavier?" Diesel asked.

"He's not you," Mackie repeated what he'd said.

Diesel lifted her up and sat her on his lap. He loved on Mackie like he had been waiting a lifetime for this very moment. His hands explored her body while she did the same. Diesel kissed her entire body from head to toe. Mackie was enjoying being pampered. She didn't think her nipples could get any harder but when Diesel slid her toes into his mouth and begun sucking them, the tingling intensified.

Diesel didn't know how Mackie would feel about all of this in the morning, but for tonight, he planned to show her what she had been missing all of these years. He worked his way up to her vagina. When he reached it, he buried his head there. It was a place he never wanted to leave. He put his hands under her ass and lifted her body to give him deeper access. When his tongue slid in, Mackie exploded immediately; the wetness and thickness of his tongue hit her walls just right. He delved deeper. With each thrust of his tongue, Mackie pulled his head closer to her pussy. If she could have stuck his entire head inside of her, she would have. Mackie screamed out in pleasure as her body shook from being eaten out like she had the best tasting pussy in the world.

"Come here," Mackie told him. Diesel climbed up next to Mackie. She laid down on top of him. "Just hold me," she told him. They both dozed off within minutes.

***

Khalil pulled up to the Preston Wood house. Blaze had sent him to check on Diesel and Mackie. Neither were answering their phones. Blaze was getting ready to drive over himself, but Khalil told him he wasn't far from it. "I'll call you when I get there," he'd told Blaze.

"Both their cars are here," Khalil told Blaze over the phone. I'm going in. I'll have Mackie to call you."

"No, tell Diesel to call me. Mackie is pissed with me right now," Blaze told him.

"Alright," Khalil responded.

Khalil took his gun from the hidden compartment in his car before walking to the door. He would always be safe before being sorry. He used his own set of keys to open the front door. Everything looked normal from what he could tell. He checked the three front rooms before walking into the master bedroom. There they were. Mackie laid out on top of Diesel with all her ass hanging out.

"Dude, Blaze is gone fuck you up," Khalil said.

Both Mackie and Diesel jumped up.

"Shit, is Blaze here?" Diesel asked. Mackie rushed into the bathroom.

"No," Khalil turned his head. He had no desire to see either one of them naked. "Man, when you get dressed, I'll be in the living room."

Mackie came back out of the bathroom with a robe on. She smiled at Diesel.
Diesel didn't smile back.

"Oh come on, you know this is funny," Mackie said.

"For you maybe. You've got big brother wrapped around your little finger," Diesel told her.

Mackie grabbed his hand pulling him into the living room. Diesel sat in a chair and Mackie flopped down on his lap.

"Really y'all?" Khalil asked.

"Yes, why?" Mackie snapped.

"How long have y'all been knowing each other?"

"It doesn't matter." Mackie was doing all the talking.

Khalil shook his head. "Diesel, Blaze wants you to call him. He's been trying to reach y'all. Now I know why y'all weren't answering the damn phone."

Mackie and Diesel looked at their phones sitting on the coffee table.

"What's up?" Diesel asked Khalil. He was starting to get paranoid thinking Blaze knew what just happened between him and Mackie.

"Don't worry yet. It's about business," Khalil smirked.

"Well if it's about business, why didn't he ask me to call him?" Mackie asked.

Khalil sighed. He didn't have time for their guilty feeling asses. "Because y'all just got into it earlier and he knew you wouldn't want to talk to him."

"Oh," Mackie said.

Diesel didn't respond. He was pissed at himself for not staying strong with Mackie like Blaze had suggested. They had too much going on right now for them to be testing out a new relationship. And to make matters worse, Khalil had basically caught them in the act. Khalil told Blaze everything. It would only be a matter of hours before he would be telling Blaze what he walked in on.

"Look Khalil, can you not say anything to Blaze about what you just saw. I want to talk to him myself first," Diesel requested.

Khalil made him stew for a minute before saying, "Alright. You've got a day. After that, I have to let him know what's going on. No secrets in the organization. You know that."

"Well damn, y'all act like I'm not sitting right here. Blaze is not my damn daddy. I can get with whoever the hell I want to," Mackie vented.

Neither Diesel nor Khalil acknowledged what she said. They both knew that Blaze let her think she was running shit. But when times get rough, Blaze handled shit.

CHAPTER TWENTY-ONE
KEYA

Keya was back at the hospital sitting next to Xavier's bed. Khalil had been true to his word. He came back at about 6:55 to take her to dinner. She'd enjoyed the company and also finally having someone other than Xavier, Aleah, and her co-workers to talk with. Keya let Khalil steer the conversation. She didn't want to bring up anything that he didn't feel comfortable talking about. But to her surprise, he told her more about himself than she expected.

Khalil had grown up in Houston's Sunnyside neighborhood before moving to Dallas when he was a teenager. Sunnyside was just as bad as Dallas' Joppa neighborhood. Sunnyside ranked the sixth most dangerous neighborhood in the United States. Most of the kids living in Sunnyside have no hope or ambition. When Khalil's mom saw him losing his drive for making something of his life, she packed up and moved to Dallas. His mom had no clue where to go in Dallas. She chose south Dallas because that's where she could afford an apartment. Without knowing, she had jumped out of the frying pan and into the fire.

It didn't take long for Khalil to start making runs for the neighborhood drug gang. It offered him the quick money that he needed to help his mom and buy all the things that he wanted. The only stipulation that he had for the gang was that he worked alone. After they saw his work ethic, he moved up the ranks quickly. When

Blaze needed someone laid back that matched his own personality, he pulled Khalil into his inner circle.

Keya only told Khalil that her parents had died when she was young; no details. Xavier had seen to it that she finished school and went to college. They had no other living family members that they knew of. Their parents had cut ties with everyone because of her father's abusive personality. They were all each other had. It made sense now knowing how protective she was of her brother. It was almost the same situation with Mackie and Blaze.

"I guess that's something that you and Mackie have in common," Khalil had said. "Blaze and Mackie lost their parents, too, and he raised Mackie."

Keya was surprised to learn this new information. The sound of the blood pressure machine broke Keya's thoughts up.

"Xavier, you have to wake up," Keya spoke to him. "I need you to fight. I can't stay in this world by myself. I have so much to tell you. And if you and Aleah want to get a divorce, that's fine too. You should both be happy. Life is too short to not be with someone who makes you happy." Keya laid her head down on Xavier's bed.

She prayed. "Dear Heavenly Father, please come into this room right now Lord. Touch Xavier's body Lord. Make him whole again. God, you said that you were my shepherd and that I shall not want. That means that I can depend on you to answer my call. So I'm asking you Lord, wake Xavier up. Let him be restored to the man that he used to be. Amen."

Keya felt a little better after praying. She remembered what her grandmother used to say, "If you pray, don't worry and if you worry, don't pray." She was going to try her best not to worry.

As soon as Keya finished praying, Xavier's doctor walked in. Keya knew him from when he used to work in the emergency room before moving to the intensive care unit. "Hey Doc," she greeted. "I was hoping to see you. How are things looking for Xavier?"

Keya watched as he diverted his eyes. It was a sign that things were not looking good.

"It's still pretty early to make any concrete statements about his recovery," the doctor stated.

"Look Doc, I want you to be brutally honest with me. I need to know if my brother is going to recover from this or not," Keya demanded.

"Things were looking really good before earlier today. What ever happened caused him to have a major setback," he told her.

Keya allowed a tear to fall from her eye. *If I hadn't argued with Mackie this wouldn't have happened*, she thought. "She really was just there trying to visit him," Khalil had told her.

"Xavier is experiencing a condition called anoxic brain injury. It resulted from him having a heart attack. We were pretty sure that the bullet didn't graze his heart, so having an attack like he did is a little shocking."

"How are you planning to treat him?" Keya asked.

"Well I'm sure that you know the longer he stays in a coma, the worse it becomes for his prognosis," the doctor stated.

Keya shook her head in agreement.

"The response time was very quick so there was not an enormous amount of time that he had a lack of oxygen. But still so, anytime the brain is deprived of oxygen you lose brain cells. Right now we are at a wait and see point. We are hoping that with him being on a ventilator, the brain will do what it's supposed to do naturally. If the swelling to his brain doesn't go down by tomorrow, we are going to have to perform surgery to remove any excess fluid that's gathered."

Keya felt like she was going to lose her mind. It was too much for her to bear alone. She didn't have Xavier. She didn't have Aleah. She didn't have anybody. The doctor could see that Keya was almost at her breaking point.

"Keya, is there anybody that I can call for you?"

"No," was all that she could get out before bursting into tears.

The doctor called for the nurse to help Keya back to the waiting room. She stayed with Keya. Her tears slowly started to subside. Keya's chest was still heaving up and down. She was thinking about the fact that Xavier may never fully recover from this. The doctor didn't say that, but she had been around enough coma patients to know what types of battles they would be facing. Xavier could possibly live in a vegetative state for the rest of his life. That thought set off another round of tears.

"Oh God," she cried. "Is this Xavier's punishment for his cruel treatment of Aleah? You're a good God. All that's good and perfect comes from you. You don't do karma, remember," Keya continued talking to her Lord and Savior.

The nurse tried her best to console Keya, but the more she said, the harder Keya cried. She used her phone to call for Damien. She knew that Damien and Keya were friends. When Damien walked up, Keya collapsed into his arms. She was practically hysterical and mumbling incoherently. No one could make out what she was saying.

Damien told the nurse to go get a sedative. It would help calm Keya down and reduce her irritability. When the nurse brought the sedative back and a cup of water, Damien had to give it her like she was child. He placed the pill on her mouth and forced her to drink and swallow. He was able to get Aleah to a private room where they admitted her for observation. Damien really felt that she only needed some rest. She had been at the hospital all day and all night. There was only so much rest that you could get at a hospital. But trying to get her to leave would be like trying to pry a steak from a pit bull's mouth.

CHAPTER TWENTY-TWO
ALEAH

Aleah was having the best sex of her life. When Blaze told her he was going to show her how a real man made love to a real woman, he wasn't lying. But truth be told, they had passed the lovemaking stage over an hour ago. Now they were just downright fucking. Blaze acted like he was trying to fuck her brains out, and she was determined to match his pace. The way Blaze had her body feeling, she didn't ever want it to stop.

Aleah was pissed when they had to take a quick break. Khalil had called to tell Blaze something about a police officer asking questions about Mackie. While he was on the phone, Aleah went into the bathroom to take a quick shower. She had sweated so much that she wanted to get fresh for Blaze again. Aleah was glad that she did because once Blaze finished his phone call, he walked into the bathroom to join her in the shower.

Aleah loved looking at the sight of his body. Blaze was toned on every part of his chiseled body. The most magnificent piece of his body, hands down was his penis. It looked like one of the pictures that you and your girlfriends forward to each other, oohing and awing over. *And right now, it's all mine*, Aleah thought.

Blaze stepped into the shower. Aleah immediately wrapped her hands around his dick that was already pointing at her. She started with a slow motion, working her hand up and down his shaft. Blaze allowed her to work her magic. He enjoyed the feel of the water tap dancing against his skin. He used his forefingers to trace small circles around Aleah's nipples. The sensation caused her to lose her rhythm. Blaze used it as opportunity to take control. He turned Aleah around and moved her forward, so that she was standing directly under the square rainfall faucet. Blaze slowly increased the water temperature. He waited a few minutes each time that he increased it, to allow her body time to adjust to the hotness of the water. When it reached a heat that he thought was close to her threshold, he dropped to his knees and began teasing between her folds.

Aleah didn't know if it was love or lust, but she wanted to be with this man for the rest of her life. When Blaze felt like she was ready to explode, he stopped.

"Don't stop," Aleah begged. Blaze smiled.

"I want to be inside you," Blaze nibbled on her nipple as he stood up.

"Ok," Aleah giggled.

Blaze leaned her over so that her hands rested on the shower bench. He took his time sliding in to her. He'd learned a long time ago that with his size, he had to take his time entering women or they'd be screaming for dear life. Once he was in, he picked up his pace.

"That feels so good," Aleah moaned. She turned her body over to Blaze to allow him to have his way with her. She trusted him to please her any way that he saw fit. As Aleah moans became louder, Blaze pumped harder. He held her by her waist to keep her steady while he drilled as deep and hard as he could.

"Oh…my…" Aleah stuttered. "I'm about to cum."

"Let it go baby," Blaze told her. "Cum all over this dick."

Aleah howled out in pleasure as her juices saturated Blaze.

Blaze wasn't finished yet. He traded places with Aleah, sitting down on the bench. He pulled Aleah down on top of him and helped her grind her hips on top of him. Blaze made good use of his hands and mouth, as he worked them to bring Aleah's nipples to life.

Blaze loved sliding his tongue across her nipples. They were the biggest he had ever seen when she was aroused.

Blaze picked Aleah up, stepped from the shower, and carried her back to the bed. He positioned her on the end so that he could enter her from behind once again. This time, he took pleasure in slapping her ass while his dick was lodged deep inside of her. The slaps to her ass hurt like hell, but felt good at the same time. Finally, Blaze was about to climax. His breathing increased right along with his strokes. He growled as he released his semen into Aleah. They collapsed on the bed, both spent from hours of lovemaking and fucking. Blaze kissed her on the cheek and pulled the covers up over their bodies. Both were asleep within minutes.

Aleah and Blaze were wakened a little while later by the ringing of her cell phone.

"Hello," Aleah said groggily into the receiver.

"Hi, this is Nurse Damien calling from Methodist Hospital. I'm trying to reach Aleah Thomas."

"This is Aleah."

"Hi Mrs. Thomas. I'm calling because your sister-in-law, Keya, had a panic attack. We gave her a sedative to help her rest. She's been admitted, but only for observation. You were listed as the next of kin on her human relations file."

Aleah sat up in the bed as soon as the nurse mentioned Keya's name.

After he finished with giving her all the details, she asked, "What room is she in?

"Room 210," Damien told her.

"Thanks, I'm on my way," Aleah told him.

"What's going on?" Blaze asked.

"Keya had a panic attack at the hospital. They admitted her. I need to go see her. With Xavier in a coma, she doesn't have anybody else," Aleah explained. Aleah hoped that he understood why she needed to be there.

"I'll drive you," Blaze told her.

Aleah smiled. *He just keeps getting better and better*, she thought.

"You don't have to," Aleah told him. "I have my car outside."

"I want to," he responded.

"Are you sure, you haven't had much rest since you were released?"

"I'm sure. But I won't go into her room with you. She hates me," Blaze stated.

"She just hasn't gotten a chance to know you like I have," Aleah told him.

Aleah leaned back placing a kiss on Blaze's lips.

"I can get used to this," she told him.

CHAPTER TWENTY-THREE
MACKIE

Diesel picked up the phone and dialed Blaze's number.

"Hey Diesel. I've been trying to reach you. Khalil just told me about some shit that's going down and I need you to secure Mackie for me. All the arrangements have been made. I just need you to get to the checkpoints in a timely matter and stay with her until I call for y'all. It could be a couple of weeks or a couple of months. I'm not sure. I know Mackie is going to give you some slack about it and will probably refuse to go, but I need you to make this happen," Blaze told him.

"Ok," Diesel responded. He got up to get a pencil and paper. He wrote down all the information that he needed.

Blaze continued giving instructions and details. "Since it's going to be a while, you can take your girl Shay with you, and your son. Just remember not to talk shop business in front of her."

"I think I'll roll solo on this one. Just give me a few hours to swing by and see my son. After that, we'll be out," Diesel agreed.

"Ok, let me holla at Khalil," Blaze said.

Diesel tossed the phone to Khalil. He told Khalil to stay with Mackie until Diesel got back.

When he hung up the phone, Mackie had a million questions. She wanted to know who, what, why, where, when and how. Both Khalil and Diesel were vague in their responses. They left her with the impression that they were going to meet with a new connect and the new connect had only wanted to deal with her. Diesel thought of the lie on the spot and Khalil co-signed everything he said.

"I need to go see my son," Diesel said. "When I get back, be ready to roll."

Mackie didn't respond. She had never been the jealous type, but she knew going to see his son meant going to see Shay. She didn't know how she felt about that.

Khalil felt the tension in the room. He stood and walked from the room. This was the type of shit that he knew wasn't good for the organization. *Don't get your honey where you make your money*, he thought.

As soon as he left the room, Diesel asked, "What's wrong?" although he already had a good idea.

"You're going to see Shay," Mackie responded.

"I am going to see my son," Diesel stated.

"Whose mom happens to be your girl," Mackie told him.

"Whose mom *used* to be my girl," Diesel corrected.

He turned her head towards him and kissed her lips.

"Mackie, I have been in love with you since we were in high school. Shay was just a substitute because I couldn't have you. I know that may sound harsh, but I have always known what Shay was all about. I was her backup plan when she couldn't get Blaze to fuck her. But I slipped up and got her pregnant. So I stayed with her out of convenience and having easy access to my son. She doesn't love me. She uses me for what I can provide for her. The only thing that scares her is the thought of losing me and losing the weekly cash that I give her."

That made Mackie feel better. She always thought that Diesel didn't know what type of chick Shay was. She thought that he was really in love with her.

"Where are we going?" Mackie asked.

"We are going to drive down to the border, cross over into Mexico and then take a flight to Grand Cayman," Diesel told her.

"What kind of connect is set up in the Cayman Islands?" she asked.

"I'm not sure. It's probably just a safe meeting point," Diesel lied.

"I've never been to the beach. Do you think we can spend a little time on the beach while we are there?" Mackie was getting excited.

"Your wish is my command," Diesel stated. He stood up and Mackie stood as well. "Don't pack anything, we'll shop when we get there."

"Ok," Mackie responded.

Diesel pulled her close. He grabbed her ass while looking into her eyes. "Am I dreaming?"

Mackie stretched up placing a kiss on his lips. They kissed for so long that Khalil walked back in, clearing his throat. When he no longer heard them talking, he thought that it was safe for him to come back into the room.

"Oh what a tangled web we weave when we first practice to deceive," Khalil said.

"Shut up Khalil," Mackie told him.

Khalil laughed. The shit was actually kind of funny to him. These two have known each other since childhood and now after umpteen years, they want to start a relationship. *Get the fuck out of here with that,* he thought.

***

Diesel drove over to Shay's crib. He wasn't looking forward to dealing with Shay at all but he couldn't leave town without letting his son know that he loved him and was going to miss him. Blaze said it could possibly be months before he and Mackie could come back to town.

Diesel let a sigh, opened the car door and walked to Shay's front door. Somehow he didn't feel right using the key that she had given him to her place. Diesel always felt like she gave it to him to make him believe that he could trust her and had access to come into her house anytime he wanted.

Diesel chose to knock on the door rather than using the key. When Shay looked through the peephole, she saw that it was Diesel. Diesel had heard her footsteps coming to the door, but she didn't open it right away. He knocked again wondering why she hadn't opened the door. After about seven minutes, she opened the door yawning like she'd just woken up.

When Diesel walked in, it smelled like sex. *Somebody has been in here fucking*, he thought.

"Hey baby," Shay said as she tried to hug him. "I didn't expect you to come home tonight."

Diesel sidestepped her arms as she was reaching for him.

Really, he couldn't care less who was laying up between Shay's legs, but he didn't want his son exposed to trifling shit.

"Where's Lil' Man," Diesel asked?

"He's still at my mom's, why?"

Shit. Diesel wished he would have called first. It could have saved him time. There was no way that he was going to Shay's mother's house. She was a psycho bitch that hated Diesel. She'd wanted Diesel to marry Shay when she got pregnant. She had started planning a wedding and telling all of her friends that he and Shay were getting married. When he finally shut her down sternly, she cussed him up and down, forward to back and inside out. They hadn't clicked since that day. But she was a great grandmother to his son, so Diesel tolerated her.

"I'm going out town for a few months, I wanted to see him before I left," Diesel told her.

"Where are you going?" Shay asked with attitude.

"Down south," he answered. He would never tell Shay about anything to do with the business.

"For what?"

"Its business," Diesel answered.

"Oh, so you going with Mack Bitch?"

"Watch ya' mouth," Diesel told her.

"I ain't got to watch my mouth. Hell, your ass has been gone, missing in action, probably laid up with her ass and then you come in her telling me y'all going out town."

"It's business," Diesel repeated.

"Ok, well I want to go. Me and Lil' Man," Shay said. "We can make it a family thing."

"You're not going," Diesel said as he looked towards the bedroom. It sounded like someone had stomped their toe and was wincing in pain.

"Who's in the room?" Diesel asked.

Shay looked uncomfortable. "Nobody," she stuttered.

Diesel pulled out his gun. "If it's nobody, then somebody is trespassing." He stood up and walked to the bedroom door with Shay pulling on his arm.

"Diesel," she repeated several times.

Diesel kicked the door open when he reached it. There one of his soldiers stood butt ass naked, trying to put his clothes back on. Diesel pointed the gun at him.

"Diesel, man, I didn't know Shay was your girl. She didn't tell me that."

"Shut up Tyson," Shay yelled.

"She's not my girl, Ty. You can fuck her anytime you want to." He put his gun back in his waistband. "The bitch just gave me a son. That's all."

"Fuck you Diesel," Shay spat. "You're just mad because somebody else wants this pussy that you couldn't handle."

Diesel burst out laughing. "Shay, now that's some funny shit." He continued laughing. "Your pussy is just mediocre." He stopped laughing just as suddenly as he had started and spoke. "Now tonight I tasted some pussy that was so damn sweet that I'm going to try to have my tongue surgically attached to it."

Shay charged at him swinging her arms wildly. She connected slap after slap to Diesel's face, head, and arms.

"Man, get this bitch off of me," he told Tyson. Diesel had never in his life hit a woman and he wouldn't start now.

Shay struggled with Tyson trying to break free to go after Diesel again.

Diesel turned to walk towards the door.

"All you care about is Mackie and that damn Carter Empire. Well guess what, I am going to the police and I am going to tell them everything that I know. I hope all y'all asses end up in jail," Shay screamed.

Diesel turned back around. "Do that Shay, and I swear to God I will take Lil' Man and leave town. I promise you will never ever see him again."

The look in Diesel's eyes had scared Shay. She still had to play hard but she pulled way back. "Whatever," she barked.

Diesel walked out, slamming the door behind him. He was more pissed that he had wasted his time. He and Mackie could have been an hour into their drive to the border.

CHAPTER TWENTY-FOUR
BLAZE

Blaze and Aleah were on their way to the hospital. If Blaze had his way, they would have gone for another round of sexing before leaving the house. As much as Aleah wanted to, she had to make Blaze put it on hold. She knew things were tense between her and Keya right now, but she would literally drop everything to make sure that she was ok. Keya had been her support system for so long that Aleah felt like she had no choice but to try to be there for her, as much as Keya had been there for her throughout the years. *But that doesn't mean that I have to stay with Xavier,* Aleah thought. *This is all about Keya.*

Blaze and Aleah were both consumed in their own thoughts. Blaze had Mackie on his mind. He wouldn't relax until Diesel had called to say that they'd made it safely to Grand Cayman. Blaze hadn't told Diesel the truth about how long they might be in the Cayman Islands. It very well could be up to a year, depending on how fast or slow his case moved through the court system. He was pretty confident in Diesel with Mackie. He knew that if it came down to it, Diesel would gladly lay down his life for Mackie, unlike Xavier's weak ass. The further he got Mackie away from him, the better.

"Shit," Blaze said as he looked into his rearview mirror.

"What's wrong?" Aleah asked. The moment those words left Aleah's mouth, she heard the sound of a police siren. The flashing lights caused her to turn and look over her shoulder.

"Where you speeding?" she asked Blaze.

"Nope. It's the same assholes from earlier. It's become their hobby, fucking with me."

"They can't do that, I know the law," Aleah spoke. "This is harassment."

Blaze smiled at her naivety. "Aleah," he called her name softly. He wanted her undivided attention. "I need you to remain quiet. Just answer their questions with a yes or no, ok?"

Aleah heard the seriousness of his tone. She nodded her head yes.

Blaze lifted her hand and kissed it.

"Put your hands where I can see them," Blanton's voice boomed throughout the car. Blaze and Aleah held their hands up. Blanton told Blaze to get out of the car. Zamora told Aleah to get out of the car. When Aleah stepped out of the car, Zamora looked at her from head to toe. Frowning she stated, "You're cute."

"Thank you?" Aleah asked, being sarcastic.

"Aleah," Blaze called her name. She looked at him. He shook his head reminding her to remain quiet. Aleah had forgotten that quickly.

"Aleah," Zamora repeated. "Cute name too." Aleah didn't say a word this time. "Step to the end of the car," she told Aleah. Aleah moved as instructed. Blaze was on the other side of the car but he moved as well keeping his eyes on Aleah. He didn't know how far these two planned to go this time. He prayed they wouldn't fuck with Aleah.

"Blaze, do you have any guns or drugs in the car," Blanton asked.

"Nope," Blaze answered.

"Miss, have you seen any guns or drugs in the vehicle," Blanton turned to Aleah.

"No," Aleah replied.

There you go baby, Blaze winked at Aleah.

Zamora saw Blaze wink and got pissed off. "Blanton, why don't you search the car?" Blaze looked at Zamora. "I'll search these two." She licked her lips while eyeing Blaze.

"Put your hands above your head," she told Aleah.

Blaze was pissed. Zamora was going to fuck with Aleah to get at him.

Zamora slid her foot between Aleah's legs lightly, kicking them just as she had done Blaze earlier. "Spread those legs for me sweetheart," Zamora said seductively. She moved in close to Aleah, pressing her breasts into Aleah's back. Aleah's eyes bucked. Zamora moved her chest from side to side so that Aleah could feel her nipples.

"Zamora," Blaze called. "Please don't."

She didn't answer. Zamora took her hands and put them on Aleah's sides. She slid them down slowly. She reached around her body placing her hands just under Aleah's breasts.

Aleah kept her eyes glued to Blaze as she bit her bottom lip.

Zamora continued. Although she used open hands in the so called search, she brushed Aleah's breasts making contact with the backs of her hands.

Blaze closed his eyes and looked down, as a tear fell from Aleah's eye. Zamora wasn't through yet. She kept her eyes glued to Blaze as well. She wanted to send him a message. She moved her hands down to Aleah's waist. When shed slid her hands in Aleah's pockets, she whispered in her ear, "I searched your boyfriend just like this earlier today." Upon saying those last words, she groped Aleah's crotch. Aleah jumped and Blaze knew what she had done.

I'm going to fuck you up, Blaze thought. He had fire in his eyes. Aleah mouthed to him, "I'm ok." She didn't want him to get angry and go off. It wouldn't end good for him if he did.

Agent Zamora stepped back from Aleah. "This one is clean," she yelled to her partner.

"Check Blaze," he yelled back. "I know there's a hidden compartment in here somewhere."

Blaze could hear Blanton ripping up the carpet in his car. It didn't bother him at all. He could have a new car tonight if he wanted it. He had his car salesman on speed dial.

Zamora walked around the car and stood in front of Blaze. Blaze put his hands behind his back. If he didn't, he would snap her neck. "I see why you like her, she's got those nice soft tits, small round ass, and a steaming hot pussy," Zamora whispered.

The cold dark penetrating stare of Blaze's eyes and his demeanor caused Zamora to have second thoughts about fucking with him.

"He's clean," Zamora said to her partner again. She hadn't touched Blaze, but figured she had made her point anyway with Aleah.

Blanton finished trashing Blaze's car and walked back to join everyone at the back of the vehicle. He leaned in to Blaze and told him, "You can make all this stop anytime you want to, just help us get Mackie off the streets.

"Guess you two love birds can be on your way," Agent Zamora said.

Blaze stood there eyeing the both of them. They stared back. All three of them were waiting to see who blinked first. Aleah didn't want to find out.

"Blaze," she called across the trunk. "Blaze," she repeated.

Blaze didn't answer. He walked around to Aleah never taking his eyes off the two. He placed his hand on the small of her back and guided her to the front seat.

Agent Blanton and Agent Zamora laughed and walked to their car, got in and drove off. They honked as they passed them.

Blaze got in the driver's seat and yelled, "That fucking bitch put her hands on you. That bitch is about to get touched."

"Blaze, I'm ok," Aleah tried to tell him.

"She don't know who the hell she's fucking with," he continued.

Aleah reached over taking his face in her hands. She made him look at her. "I'm fine. I was shocked at first, but I'm good." She kissed him. She could feel his body start to relax. She kissed his neck. She trailed kissed all over his face.

"I'm sorry," Blaze told her. She shushed him.

"You didn't do anything that you need to apologize for," Aleah told him.

"I'm supposed to protect you. That's my job," Blaze said.

"And that's what you did. If you hadn't told me what to do, I probably would have ended up in jail or dead tonight."

"Are you sure you're ok?" Blaze asked.

"What, you didn't know? I'm your ride or die chick," Aleah tried to sound hood.

Blaze laughed. "Ok ride or die." He started the car and they continued driving to the hospital.

CHAPTER TWENTY-FIVE
MACKIE

Mackie was excited about going to Cayman. She picked up her laptop and typed in Grand Cayman in the search engine. She clicked on images and said, "Wow! This place looks amazing."

"Look," she told Khalil. He half-looked and mumbled "yeah." He was preoccupied with a PlayStation. He was playing some commando shooting game.

"Do you know what hotel we are staying at?" she asked.

"I think Blaze mentioned Motel 6," Khalil laughed.

"Shut up fool," Mackie told him.

Mackie continued looking at the beaches and the hotels. "That's it, I want to stay at the Ritz Carlton. It's right on Seven Mile Beach."

"Let me guess. Y'all want to stay in the honeymoon suite, right?" Khalil was having fun mocking their newfound relationship.

"I hadn't thought about that, but that's a good idea," Mackie replied.

Khalil shook his head.

"Don't hate Khalil. It's not cute on you. You need to get yourself a good woman to settle down with. You can't run around in the streets forever," Mackie said.

"Who the fuck am I talking to and what the hell did you do to Mackie?" Khalil acted like he was looking around the room for her.

Mackie gave him the one-finger salute.

"I can't, you're already taken," Khalil added.

Mackie laughed. "Why don't we ever get to see your fun side?"

"I don't know. Probably because I'm always taking care of business."

"Well, I'm going to make it my mission to find you somebody to love," Mackie insisted.

"Please don't," Khalil stated. Khalil started thinking about Keya. He really liked her and wondered if she could actually be the one. The only negative that he could see right now was that Xavier was her brother. From what he had heard about him from Blaze, he was foul. He couldn't understand why Mackie even gave him the time of day. *Mackie being with Diesel is definitely a step up*, he thought.

"Khalil, you should come with us to Cayman," Mackie said.

"And have to watch you and Diesel make goo-goo eyes at each other all day. Um yeah, no. I'll pass," Khalil told her.

They both laughed but jumped and grabbed their pieces when the front door opened.

"Dude, you was about to get a toe tag," Khalil stated. "Next time, you betta let a nigga know you bouncing through the door."

Diesel didn't respond. Mackie could tell he wasn't in the same mood that he was in when he'd left earlier.

"What's wrong?" Mackie asked.

"It's personal," Diesel responded.

"That's my cue," Khalil said standing. "I'm out. Y'all be careful, follow the instructions to the letter. Don't deviate. You can play when you get there. And check in periodically."

"Damn, daddy number two," Mackie stated.

"This is serious Mackie," Khalil expressed.

"Ok, I got it," Mackie looked serious. *I guess the Khalil that we know and love is back,* she thought.

Once Khalil was out of the door, Mackie turned to Diesel.

"What happened?" Mackie knew that Diesel didn't want to talk in front of Khalil.

"Shay is a bitch," he responded.

"She's always been a bitch," Mackie added.

"I didn't get to see my son. He's been at her mom's house for the last few days."

"Do you want to go see him over there?" Mackie asked.

"Naw, she's even more of a bitch than Shay is. I told Shay that I would be out of town for a while. She wanted to tag along. When I told her no, she got all whacked out. But fuck her."

"Did you tell her that I was going?"

"Yeah, that's what pissed her off," Diesel replied.

"Like you said, fuck her," Mackie added. "Is that all?"

Diesel paused trying to decide if he wanted to tell Mackie the rest of it. One thing that he didn't want is for them to keep secrets. They were already going to have to deal with Blaze. Worrying about lies and half-truths would only make things worse.

"Tyson was there when I got there, fucking Shay," Diesel blurted.

"Pleasant Grove Tyson?" Mackie asked.

"Yep," Diesel replied.

"Ain't Tyson HIV positive?" Mackie frowned.

"Yep."

"Damn, does she know?" Mackie kept the questions coming.

"I doubt it; he would never tell a bitch. Only way we know is 'cause we saw his pill bottle at the crib one day. He forgot and left it out. Me being a curious mofo', you know I looked that shit up. That's when I told you. I don't think nobody else in the crew knows," Diesel gave a reply.

"Did you tell her?" Mackie asked.

"Hell naw. If she wasn't such an asshole tonight I would have. But I'll probably call her back tomorrow or some shit and let her know she needs to get checked."

"How long do you think she's been fucking him?" Mackie wanted to know.

"I don't know," Diesel said.

"When was the last time you had sex with her?"

Diesel knew why she was asking. "About a week ago, but I always wrap my shit up with Shay. I would never slide up in her raw. She caught me drunk that one time, and Lil Man was the result. Tyson's young ass wasn't even on the block yet.

Are you ready to hit the road?" Diesel asked. He wanted to put some distance between them and Dallas real quick. He wasn't sure how serious Shay was about talking to the police. The faster he got Mackie out of the country, the better.

"More than ready! Cayman is beautiful. I looked it up while you were gone. I can't wait to get there," Mackie said. "How long is the drive to the border?"

"About six and a half hours," Diesel told her.

"Cool," Mackie stated. Normally she would have pitched a fit and asked if they could fly instead. But riding six hours in a car with Diesel sounded like fun.

Diesel had gassed the car up on his way back. They set the alarm for the house and set out for Laredo, Texas. Diesel planned to drive all night, reaching the border early the next morning.

CHAPTER TWENTY-SIX
ALEAH

Aleah was glad that she was able to calm Blaze down. She sat thinking on the rest of drive over to the hospital. She held Blaze's hand with her head resting on his shoulder. She wished that she would have never met and married Xavier. She was starting to realize how much more she deserved out of life than what he had to offer. Blaze was opening her eyes to a new perspective. He was caring, attentive, a protector. She needed him in her life. She hoped that he needed her as well.

"Hey, we're here," Blaze said.

Aleah raised up. She didn't want to leave him, but she knew she needed to make sure that Keya was okay.

"Do you know how long you are going to stay?" Blaze asked.

"Not really. It kind of depends on how she is doing. Then again, she might put my ass out."

"She won't. She needs somebody whether she wants to admit it or not," Blaze told her.

"I hope you're right. Keya has really been there for me through all of her brother's bullshit."

Blaze kissed Aleah. He got out of the car and walked around to open the passenger side door. He held his hand out for Aleah and she stood. He closed the door and pressed his body up against hers. As much as she didn't want to leave him, he didn't want her to go.

"I'll wait down here for you. Once you see how it is going, text me to let me know how long you're going to stay," Blaze said.

Aleah smiled.

"What's that smile about?" Blaze asked.

"You're my thug angel," Aleah told him.

Blaze laughed, "Thug angel, huh?"

"Yes," Aleah got serious. "And I love you."

Blaze smiled this time. He leaned in and kissed Aleah. "I love you too," he replied.

"I better get in here before you make me attack you right here in this parking lot," Aleah said.

"I don't mind one bit," Blaze responded.

"I'm sure you don't Mr. Carter," Aleah turned and walked away.

Once Aleah reached the door, she turned and waved. Blaze waved back.

Blaze turned at the sound of movement behind the car.

"How you doing thug angel?"

It was the detective investigating Xavier's shooting. Obviously, he had been listening in on Blaze and Aleah's conversation. Blaze did a quick recap of his conversation with Aleah to make sure he hadn't said anything that the detective could use against him. *I didn't*, he thought.

Blaze was getting sick of this shit. First it was Blanton and Zamora, and now this prick.

"What are you and Mr. Thomas' wife up to?" the detective asked.

"Man, what do you want?" Blaze breathed.

"Oh come on now, don't act that way. You and I are going to get to know each other real good. We might even become besties," he fucked with Blaze.

"Dude, I don't have besties," Blaze expressed.

"You sure? What about Khalil and Diesel?"

He was letting Blaze know that he had done some digging into his happenings. The detective smirked waiting for Blaze to answer.

"Those names don't ring a bell," Blaze exclaimed.

"Really," the detective uttered. "Well maybe this will ring a bell about the night Xavier Thomas was shot. When we booked you in that night, we used your prints to do a gun powder residue test. We sent off your prints for both of your hands. I bet you can guess what was missing from your prints."

Blaze didn't respond.

"Let me help you out. When I said that, you were supposed to say 'what was missing from my prints, detective?' Well, I am so glad you asked Thug," he paused, "Angel. Gun powder residue! So that tells me that somebody other than you shot Mr. Thomas."

Blaze's mind was running a mile a minute. He had no clue that they would use his fingerprints to check for gun powder on his hands.

"So Blaze, did Mrs. Thomas shoot her husband and you're trying to cover for her?"

"Is this interrogation legal?" Blaze asked.

The detective laughed. "This is just two friends talking."

"Number one, I'm not talking and number two, I don't have any friends."

The detective stared at Blaze. He hated, what he referred to as, punk ass drug dealers who thought they could operate above the law.

"Well just so you know my *not friend*, I'm asking the judge for an arrest warrant for your, um, what is she to you again?"

When Blaze didn't answer, he finished his sentence. "Aleah Thomas for the attempted murder of her husband. Now you have a good rest of the night."

Blaze remained cool until the detective got into his car and drove off.

"FUCK! GOT-DAMMIT!"

Things were getting way out of control. Blaze had the Feds and the Dallas Police Department breathing down his neck.

"Think Blaze," he said. *Glad Mackie is on her way out of the country. I should have sent Aleah too.*

Blaze paced back and forth for about fifteen minutes trying to come up with a way out of this mess for all of them. He knew that he couldn't take Aleah and disappear; not with the ankle monitor attached to his leg. They'd placed the highest quality monitor on him. There was no way for him to remove it. If he tried, the police would descend on his location within minutes. Blaze was sure that since he was out on bond and being hounded by the Feds and the police, that his ankle monitor was being watched like a hawk.

He wasn't even sure Aleah would want to go with him, especially with her trying to patch things up with her sister-in-law.

Blaze's phone started vibrating, breaking up his thoughts.

"Hey babe," he said to Aleah answering the phone.

"I'm going to stay for a while," Aleah told him.

"Ok, call me when you're ready and I'll come back and pick you up." Blaze disconnected the call and dialed Khalil's number.

"Meet me back at Preston Wood," Blaze told him.

***

Aleah walked into Keya's hospital room, nervous about how she would respond to her being there to check on her. Keya was asleep. She looked peaceful; like the little girl that Aleah had met when she and Xavier had first started dating. Keya was just starting high school. She had always been a nice girl. Aleah had watched her grow into a beautiful young woman.

"What's going on with us Keya?" Aleah mumbled.

Keya stirred at the sound of Aleah's voice. She opened her eyes. "Aleah?"

"Yes sweetie. It's me. I'm here to check on you."

Keya looked around the room trying to figure out where she was. "I'm in the hospital?" she asked.

"Yes," Aleah answered.

"Why?" Keya wanted to know.

"Because you needed a little rest."

"Xavier," Keya called, "how is he?"

"The same," Aleah answered. She had stopped by the intensive care unit before going to Keya's room.

"I'm sorry Aleah," Keya apologized.

Aleah was shocked. She hadn't expected this from Keya.

"You were right," Keya continued. "I know what Xavier has put you through. Instead of being angry, I should have been wondering what took you so long to find someone else. I was being immature. I was worried about losing both of you and having no one else in this world to depend on."

Aleah sat down on the bed. She reached her arms out to Keya. They hugged for what seemed like an eternity.

"Thank you for saying that, Keya." Aleah was genuinely happy that they could sit there and have an intelligent conversation about someone other than a doctor or nurse. "No matter what happens in this life, I will always be there for you. You don't have to ever worry about being alone.

CHAPTER TWENTY-SEVEN
BLAZE

When Blaze pulled up to the house, Khalil was already there. Blaze had passed his exit several times because he was preoccupied with what he was about to do. It was the only solution that he could come up with at the last minute. Neither Mackie nor Aleah would have to be suspects in Xavier's shooting. Blaze just needed to square away a few things first. He was sure the detective wasn't bluffing about having Aleah arrested. *The warrant for her arrest would probably be served sometime tomorrow*, he thought.

"What's up?" Khalil spoke when Blaze walked through the door.

"Shit's about to get way out of order," Blaze responded. "Have you heard from Diesel and Mackie?"

"They hit the road about an hour ago. Should be down around Ennis by now. I have them checking in every two hours," Khalil filled him in.

"That detective was waiting for me at the hospital a little while ago, when I went to drop Aleah off to visit Keya. Oh, by the way, Keya had some kind of breakdown or something. They admitted her," Blaze told him. "I know you probably want to go check on her but we need to handle this first."

Khalil had been thinking about Keya a lot. He did want to go see her, but Blaze was right; they had to handle business. *And she's got Aleah there with her*, he rationalized.

"What did the detective say?" Khalil tried to divert his attention to the matter at hand.

Blaze filled him in on what had been said.

"Damn, I didn't know they could test for residue from your fingerprints," Khalil mentioned.

Blaze continued. "After the detective said that, I looked up how long gun powder residue stays on your hands."

"What did it say?" Khalil asked.

"It depends on the type of test that's used. They have some that claims it can be detected a lot longer than it used to be able to be detected," Blaze explained. "If they arrest Aleah and test her hands, they'll know that she didn't shoot Xavier. It won't take long for them to make the connections and figure out Mackie's involvement."

Khalil was thinking that this whole situation was fucked up. He tried to concentrate so that he could help Blaze come up with a plan, but his mind kept drifting back to Keya.

"I don't want Aleah to have to spend even one hour in jail," Blaze stated.

"So what's the plan? Do you want to get her out of the country too?" Khalil asked.

"Nah, I don't think it'd be right of me to ask her to pick up and leave everything that she knows behind. It's different with Mackie. She knew very well what she was getting into with the lifestyle that we live. I think Aleah has an idea of what it is I do, but we've never talked about it. She didn't even ask a lot questions when the Feds pulled us over tonight."

"The Feds pulled y'all over?" Khalil asked.

"Yeah, the same two that came to see me when I was in jail. They pulled me over earlier today too."

"Damn," Khalil frowned.

Both of them knew if the Feds were snooping around, chances were that they already had enough shit on you to make an arrest. They were just trying to rattle you so that you could make a punk move and stick you with even more charges.

"I'm going to turn myself in and confess to shooting Xavier. Request no trial and move straight to sentencing," Blaze informed him.

"What?" Khalil was shocked. "I don't know if that's a good idea. Dude, how much time would you be facing?"

"I don't know yet; I need to talk to the attorney about that."

"There's got to be another option," Khalil said.

"It might be, but I don't have time to figure it out. I need to keep Mackie and Aleah straight," Blaze told him.

Blaze spent the next hour going over every detail of the business. He would be in charge. For how long, he wasn't sure. He told Khalil that he was hoping that Mackie would never return to the states. They'd made enough money to where she never had to step foot in the game again.

"I need to tell you something about Mackie and Diesel," Khalil said.

"I already know," Blaze responded.

"So you're ok with them sleeping together?" Khalil asked.

"Man, I don't want no details," Blaze said. "I know he's feeling her and it's just a matter before she realizes that he'd be good for her."

"She's already realized it," Khalil said.

"What do you mean?" Blaze asked.

"I walked in on them…"

"Ahhhhhh," Blaze cut him off. "I said no details."

Khalil laughed, "A'ight."

Blaze got serious. "I don't know where this is all going to end, but I need to you to hold it down with business and look after my girls. Mackie should be okay with Diesel. But I'm not sure about Aleah. If I'm locked up for a while, I don't know what she might do. I'm hoping she won't fall back into that abusive lifestyle with Xavier."

Khalil felt bad for his homie. "You know I got you, but I still think you should just take Aleah and leave the country. Y'all could meet up with Mackie and Diesel and build a nice life together in Cayman. You could still be running shit and I'd be here to carry it all out. El Chapa has been doing that shit for years. He has it down to a science. The Feds have been trying to catch up with him for years. Every time that they get close, he pulls a Houdini on their asses."

Blaze sat thinking about what Khalil was saying. It was tempting. He had always wanted to leave the game and start over new somewhere. This could be his one opportunity. He, Aleah, Mackie and Diesel could all have a fresh start.

"Let me see if Aleah is up for it," Blaze considered.

"If she is, you need to get out of town tonight," Khalil said.

"Yeah, we might be able to catch up with Diesel and Mackie." Blaze looked at his watch thinking it was time for Diesel to check in. A second later, Khalil's phone was buzzing.

Khalil answered, "What's up Diesel, how's it going?... Where are y'all?... They're in Buffalo."

Blaze interrupted, "how's Mackie?"

Khalil relayed that she was asleep.

"Let me holla at Diesel," Blaze reached for the phone.

"Hey Diesel, make sure you're running the posted speed limit. I don't need y'all to be stopped for any reason. You're running a little too fast if you are already in Buffalo."

Diesel slowed down. He had been catching himself increasing his speed when he got bored. Looking at all that land with no lights in sight was boring as hell.

"Hey Blaze, I need to talk to you about something," Diesel began.

"It can wait," Blaze stopped him. "Right now, just focus on getting Mackie safely out of the country. I'm depending on you to protect her."

Diesel paused. He was ready to let Blaze know about him and Mackie. He wanted everything out in the open. And with them being two hours away, he felt this was the perfect time. Blaze wouldn't be able to go off on him. For now, Diesel let it go. He did have a job to do.

After Blaze disconnected the phone, he told Khalil, "Let's get to the hospital to see Aleah and Keya."

CHAPTER TWENTY-EIGHT
KEYA

Keya and Aleah were sitting in her hospital bed talking. Keya's head was resting on Aleah's shoulder. Keya was debating on telling Aleah about Khalil. She finally blurted out, "I met somebody."

"You met somebody?" Aleah repeated.

"Yes," Keya answered.

"Where, when, who? You've been here at the hospital. Does he work here?"

Keya laughed at Aleah's excitement. For as long as she could remember, Aleah had been encouraging her to get out and find a man.

Keya smiled. "I did meet him here at the hospital but no, he doesn't work here."

"Who is he? What's his name?"

"Khalil," Keya stated.

"Khalil Hamilton?" Aleah questioned.

"Yes, how do you know him?" Keya wanted to know.

Aleah didn't answer.

"Oh." Keya realized she'd met him through Blaze.

"Sorry," Aleah spoke.

"No need to apologize. It's just going to take a little getting used to," Keya explained. "So where do things stand with you and Blaze?"

"Oh no Miss Lady. You will not change the subject. We were talking about your man," Aleah smiled.

"Well you've seen him. You know he is sexy as hell," Keya stated.

Aleah squealed. It felt like old times. "I'm so happy for you."

Keya stopped smiling. "How will I know if he really likes me?"

"Oh trust me honey, you'll know. When he pops up without you expecting him; when he wants to spend every moment he can with you; when he looks at you and smiles for no reason. You'll know," Aleah explained.

As if on cue, Khalil walked into the room carrying a dozen roses.

"Khalil," Keya breathed.

"Hi," Khalil spoke. "Heard you were feeling a little stressed. I decided to bring you some flowers to brighten your day."

"Thank you," Keya smiled. This was the first time that someone other than Xavier or Aleah had actually brought her some flowers. He walked over to where Keya was sitting on the bed. He leaned over, kissing her on her lips.

Aleah squealed again.

Keya and Khalil laughed.

"Aleah, Blaze is waiting for you in the visiting room," Khalil told her.

Aleah's eyes immediately went to Keya.

Keya responded, "Its ok, Leah."

"Thanks, keep an eye on her for me Khalil?" Aleah asked him.

"Absolutely," Khalil responded.

Aleah left the room to go talk with Blaze.

"Thanks for the flowers," Keya spoke. They're beautiful.

"You're beautiful," Khalil complimented her.

Keya blushed, something that she was starting to do more often since meeting Khalil.

"That's the beautiful smile that I want to see on your face every second of every minute, of every hour, of every day, of every week, of every year.

Keya laughed.

"I can go on; of every year, of every decade, of every-"

"No, no, I think I understand what you mean," Keya giggled.

"How are you really?" Khalil asked.

"I'm better," Keya answered.

"Good, because I want to get you out of this place. I want to take you somewhere so that you can relax.

"I can't. Not yet. I hope you understand. I have to make sure that my brother is going to be ok," Keya explained.

"I understand," Khalil admitted. "But as soon as you feel up to it, I want to show you what being happy is about."

Keya and Khalil embraced. It was short lived.

Aleah burst through the door. "The nurse just said that Xavier is awake."

Keya leapt from the bed. "I have to go see him." She grabbed Khalil's hand, "Come with me."

Aleah didn't know if she should go with them or not.

Khalil looked at Blaze standing in the hallway. Concern was etched across his face. They both knew what the consequences could be of Xavier waking up. He could tell everyone who actually shot him. Blaze prayed that Mackie and Diesel would make it to the border before that happened.

They all followed Keya as she led the line to the intensive care unit. When they reached the secured doors, Keya pressed the button and walked through with Khalil. "I'll be back to give you an update," she told Aleah.

"Ok," Aleah responded.

Blaze used this time as an opportunity to talk to Aleah about his plan. "I want you to go away with me."

"Where?" Aleah asked.

"Grand Cayman," Blaze responded.

"When?"

Blaze paused. "Tonight."

"For how long?" Aleah wanted to know.

"I'm not sure," Blaze answered truthfully.

Aleah didn't respond.

Blaze wanted to tell her more. If he was asking her to move to another country with him, she at least needed to know why.

"Remember the night that Xavier was shot. You asked me what type of work I did?"

Aleah remembered.

"I only told you half of the truth," Blaze explained. "I do run my family's business. A drug business." Blaze had expected Aleah to be shocked, but she just listened. He continued.

"My family has been doing this for as long as I can remember. It's a generational thing. I never wanted to be a part of it, but it just kind of fell upon me when my parents died. But long story short, those agents that pulled us over earlier have me on their radar, which means it's only a matter of time before they serve me with a warrant. Not to mention, this mess with Xavier being shot. I have always wanted to leave this city and this life behind. And I feel like if I don't do it right now, I might not get another chance."

Blaze was talking nonstop. Aleah couldn't have gotten a word in if she wanted.

"Aleah, I love you and I want to be with you. But I can't do it living here. I know it's a lot to ask of you so if you say no, I'll understand. Will you move with me to Cayman?"

Aleah was about to answer when Blaze's phone buzzed. It was a text from Khalil: Get Aleah out of here NOW!

Blaze grabbed Aleah's hand and pulled her as fast as he could to the stairway. He didn't know what was going on, but Khalil never overreacted and was always on point. He followed the instructions and would find out the details later.

"What's wrong?" Aleah asked.

"I'll fill you in in a minute. Right now, just trust me," Blaze relayed.

They took the stairs down two at a time. Blaze was glad that she worked out; it allowed her to keep up with his quick pace. When they reached the bottom of the stairs, Blaze peeked out to see if he saw security or the police. He did. Two security guards were scrambling towards the elevators. Blaze waited until the elevator doors closed. "Come on," he told Aleah. They sprinted across the lobby and out the front door of the hospital.

CHAPTER TWENTY-NINE
XAVIER

Keya was on cloud nine. She had Khalil by her side. She and Aleah were no longer fighting and when she walked into Xavier's room, his eyes were open. She walked over to his bed.

"X," Keya called. "You're awake."

"So are you," Xavier replied.

Keya laughed. She was glad that he was trying to crack a joke. It was a good sign.

"How are you feeling?" Keya asked.

"Tired, sore," he answered.

"That's totally expected. I'm so glad you woke up."

"What happened? Why am I in the hospital?" Xavier didn't remember.

"You were shot," Keya explained.

Xavier saw Khalil walk in with Keya, but he had a million thoughts running through his head. He finally asked, "Who are you?"

"I'm Khalil. I'm a friend of Keya's," Khalil answered.

"I don't know you," Xavier stated.

Keya tried to cut Xavier off. "Xavier, you don't know everybody that I know."

Here we go with another overprotective brother, Khalil thought. *Too bad you didn't think enough of your wife to protect her like this.*

"What do you want?" Xavier asked him.

"Xavier, stop it. He's my friend and I asked him to come in here with me," Keya fussed.

"Where is Aleah?" Xavier asked.

"She's across the hall in the waiting room," Aleah responded.

"Where is Mackie?" he asked.

Sick ass bastard, Khalil thought. *Asking about your wife and your side chick almost in the same breath.*

"I don't know," Keya answered.

"Has she been here to see me?" Xavier wanted to know.

Keya sighed. Although she didn't press charges against Mackie for hitting her, she still didn't want her with Xavier.

"Yes," Keya told him. "She was here yesterday."

"I want to see her," Xavier requested.

Damn, Khalil thought. *This motherfucker remembers. He's about to tell the world that Mackie shot him.*

"I don't know how to get in touch with her," Keya told him.

"Get my phone, her number is saved in it," Xavier instructed.

"Don't you want to see Aleah?" Keya tried to divert his attention away from wanting to see Mackie.

Xavier closed his eyes. He slowly shook his head. Keya knew that he was thinking.

Xavier opened his eyes. He looked at Keya. Hate burned in his eyes. "Hell no. She's fucking Mackie's brother, Blaze."

Keya looked at Khalil. Khalil was wondering where he was going with this. He hated Aleah. That much was obvious. But when he mentioned Mackie, his tone softened.

"I know," Keya stated.

"You know? How long have you known that my wife was fucking around Keya?" Xavier barked.

"Don't yell at her," Khalil interrupted. He hated his self-righteous ass.

"Nigga, that's my sister," Xavier replied.

"Yes, and you will respect her," Khalil added.

"Khalil," Keya called his name softly. She was feeling good at the fact that Khalil was trying to protect her, but now wasn't the time with Xavier just regaining consciousness. Khalil took a few steps back.

"Thank you," Keya mouthed the words to Khalil. "I didn't find out about it until after you had been shot," she turned her attention back to Xavier.

"Bitch," Xavier mumbled.

"Prick," Khalil mumbled.

"What did you say?" Xavier asked Khalil.

"He didn't say anything," Keya budded in. "Xavier, how can you be mad at Aleah when you were sleeping with Mackie?"

Xavier looked shocked. He knew Keya knew they had been spending time together, but she didn't know that they were sleeping together.

"Mackie is my friend. Just like this nigga is your friend," Xavier glared at Khalil.

Keya was getting pissed. Xavier was acting like he hadn't done anything wrong. *How much shit did he expect Aleah to put up with?*

"Xavier, I saw a video of you and Mackie screwing on the balcony at your company's condo."

"What video?" Xavier asked.

Shit, Keya thought. She hadn't meant to let that bit of information slip out.

"What video?" Xavier raised his voice.

This time Khalil didn't say anything about him yelling at Keya. He wanted to know more about this video too. A video floating around of Xavier and Mackie fucking wasn't good. Blaze would be pissed. Not to mention Diesel.

"You don't remember what happened?"

Xavier didn't answer.

Guess I have no choice but to spill it now, Keya thought. "Aleah went looking for you that night that you took Mackie out to eat. She tracked your phone to the condo. She started recording a woman and man having sex on the balcony. At first she didn't know who it was. But then she saw your face. It was very clear on the video."

Xavier was once again pissed off. He hated Aleah. *Stupid bitch.* "And she couldn't wait to run and show you this video, right?"

"No, that's not what happened. She hadn't planned on showing it to me at all. But we ended up getting into it after you got shot. I was accusing her of a lot of stuff that I shouldn't have been. That's when she showed me the video."

"That's some fucked up shit," Xavier exclaimed. "I can't believe she did some shit like that."

This asshole was cheating on his wife, got caught and then wants to blame her. Khalil didn't want to spend another minute in the room with him, but he needed to see where Xavier's head was.

Xavier got quiet. He looked like he was in deep thought. He remembered the night that he was shot. He had heard Blaze tell Mackie to leave and that he would handle everything with the police. She left. *Think, think.* Xavier was trying to remember what happened next. He heard Aleah's voice. He heard Blaze. *"Dial 911, tell them your boyfriend just shot your husband,"* Blaze had told Aleah. *Aleah went along with the lie. She helped Blaze cover for Mackie,* Xavier remembered. *Why would she cover for Mackie knowing that I was sleeping with her?* Xavier's face contorted into a frown. *She did it for Blaze because she's in love with him,* he figured. *Bitch gets what she gets.*

"Why is Aleah over in the waiting room and not in jail?" Xavier asked.

Keya was confused. "Jail? Why would she be in jail?" Keya asked.

"For shooting me, she tried to kill me," Xavier told her.

"WHAT!" Keya was shocked. "Aleah didn't shoot you Xavier, Blaze did."

Khalil listened to Xavier lie to Keya without an ounce of remorse or guilt. He knew where this was leading. He pulled out his phone and texted Blaze, telling him to get Aleah out of the hospital.

"No," Xavier continued. "He's covering for Aleah. She shot me. And I want her arrested and thrown in jail."

"Xavier," Keya tried to ask him more questions. "Why would Aleah shoot you?"

"Blaze and I were fighting and when she saw that I was handling his ass, she pulled the gun and shot me. Now call the police," Xavier demanded.

When Keya turned to look at Khalil, it pissed Xavier off. He pushed the nurse's button. Within a few seconds, the nurse was walking into the room.

"Call the police," Xavier told her. "I remember who shot me. It was my wife, Aleah Thomas."

The nurse ran from the room, no doubt making her way to the phone to call the police as Xavier had requested.

"Are you sure that Aleah is the one who shot you?" Khalil asked.

"That's what I said," Xavier griped.

The hospital's security team walked into Xavier's room. "Mr. Thomas, you requested for some assistance?" they asked.

"Hell no, I requested the damn police."

"Xavier, calm down," Keya pleaded.

"I'll calm down when that bitch is arrested."

"Mr. Thomas, we've called the police, but it's the hospital's policy to have their own security team to keep report of what's happening anytime the police are called," the security guard explained.

"You want a report? Report this, my fucking wife tried to fucking kill me."

CHAPTER THIRTY
MACKIE

Mackie and Diesel had been driving for almost four hours. Mackie had slept for most of it. Thanks to a huge pothole in the road, she was now wide awake.

"Are you going to stop anywhere, anytime soon?" Mackie asked.

"I hadn't planned on it. I want to get to the border, cross it and then we can grab a bite to eat before we catch the plane," Diesel answered.

"I have to use the bathroom," Mackie mentioned.

There's a plastic container in the back seat that you can use.

Mackie looked at Diesel as if he had lost his damn mind. "I am not peeing in a plastic container."

Diesel had no plans of stopping this late at night in any of these redneck ass Texas towns.

Texas towns were notorious for jacking niggas up for no other reason than to be entertained.

"Mackie, you have no choice. I can't stop. If I do, we might miss our flight to Cayman." Diesel didn't want to say that he was scared to stop, but unlike Mackie, he paid attention to the number of blacks being killed by police officers.

Mackie sighed heavily.

Sigh all you want, just climb ya ass in the backseat, Diesel thought with a chuckle.

Mackie unlocked her seatbelt and started climbing in the backseat. There was plenty of room for her to do it easily, but since Diesel was making her pee in the car, she decided to make it hard on him.

Mackie pulled her legs into the seat and turned to the side so that she was sitting on her feet. She used her arms to squeeze her breasts together. She pushed herself up and over towards him, placing her breasts right next to his head. When Diesel looked to the side to see what she was doing, he was met with a face full of titties. Diesel swerved the car. Mackie fell back into her seat.

"Diesel," she screamed.

"Sorry, somebody was distracting me," Diesel laughed as he straightened the car back up.

"You did that on purpose," Mackie told him.

"Girl, you have no idea what your body does to me," Diesel responded.

Mackie smiled at the compliment. "What does my body do to you?" Mackie asked.

Diesel looked over at her. He took her hand in his and pulled it to his lips. He softly kissed the back of her hand and then lowered it to rest on his penis.

"Oh," Mackie giggled. Diesel was as hard as a brick.

Mackie licked her lips as she began to massage Diesel's dick.

"If you want me to lose my concentration, swerve this car and land us in a ditch, just keep doing what you're doing," Diesel stated.

Mackie didn't stop. She leaned over, never removing her hand from his crotch or slowing down her motion, and started kissing Diesel's neck. Diesel shivered at the sensation. Mackie had a nice rhythm going. She was just as horny as she was making Diesel.

"Shit," Diesel uttered. Mackie and Diesel noticed the red and blue flashing lights behind them, almost at the same time. Mackie slid back over to her seat. Diesel put his blinkers on to pull the car over to the side of the road.

"We're going to visit my grandmother in Houston. She's sick. Answer all questions with a yes or no. Don't elaborate. If it's something you're not sure about, say I don't know." This car is clean. It was Mackie's SUV that she hadn't driven since she drove if home from the dealership. "This should be just a simple seat belt ticket. We're good," Mackie instructed Diesel.

Diesel knew all this. He had it down to a science, but he listened to her intently. That was one of the things that Diesel loved about Mackie. She would take control. She almost sounded like the old Mackie, before she shot Xavier and got soft.

Two Texas State Troopers approached the SUV. They flanked each side of the vehicle. Both had their guns drawn.

As the officers got closer, Diesel and Mackie breathed a little sigh of relief. Both of the officers were black. At least they didn't have to worry about racist officers trying to throw their weight around.

The troopers tapped the back of the SUV with their hand. "We need both of you to exit the vehicle slowly, with your hands in the air."

Both Mackie and Diesel did as they were instructed. Diesel was first to exit the car. When Mackie stood and turned towards the officer on her side of the SUV, he was blown away.

"Damn," he blurted.

Mackie knew she looked good. She was use to this reaction from people that didn't know who she was. Mackie had her hair pulled into a high ponytail resting on the top of her head, with cascading curls flowing down, touching her shoulder. The hairstyle pulled back on her eyes causing her to look even more exotic than she already did. She wore a pair of cotton leggings and a cut crop top, showing off her D-sized cups.

The officer lowered his gun and re-holstered it. He stared at Mackie. Mackie smiled seductively. It wouldn't be the first time or last that she used her good lucks to get what she wanted. And the last thing that she and Diesel needed was being tied to some backwards ass town in the form of a ticket.

"What?" his partner asked.

Mackie winked at the officer.

"Nothing," he responded.

Diesel was trying to get a look at what was going on with Mackie and the officer, but couldn't see because the height of the SUV.

When the officer standing by Diesel saw him looking in Mackie's direction, he asked him to turn in the opposite direction. Diesel was pissed but followed his instructions. They didn't need any complications.

Mackie heard the officer telling Diesel to turn around. She knew that he couldn't see what was going on. She was appreciative. Mackie did her signature sexy sway towards the officer. "What's the problem sir?" she spoke.

"When you drove by us, we noticed you didn't have your seatbelt on. You were almost in the seat with the driver. It seemed that you might have been distracting him from the way that the car was swaying. Looking at you now, you could have been in the passenger seat with the seatbelt on and still would have been distracting him."

"I think that's a compliment," Mackie responded. "Thank you."

"You're welcome. You are one sexy bitch," the officer stated.

Mackie wondered if she had heard him wrong. "What?" She had to control her temper. Her pet peeve was being called a bitch. She knew that some women used it as a "my girl" type thing, but Mackie could never get with that silliness. When she used the word bitch to refer to someone, she meant it in the old school way and you best believe wasn't nothing nice about it.

The officer noticed Mackie's frown at being called a bitch. "I'm sorry, I just meant that you look damn good to me. What's your name?" he asked.

"Mackenzie," she said.

"I like that, Kenzie," he stated. "Where are you from?"

"Dallas," she answered.

"D-Town." He was trying way too hard to impress Mackie.

"So what am I being charged with?" Mackie smiled.

"I can think of a whole lot of things," he flirted. He wanted to get a chance to look at Mackie's ass. "I need to see your identification."

"It's in my purse," Mackie replied turning around to get it.

"Gottttt dammmmn," the trooper stated.

Mackie was leaning in the car, giving him a nice view her rump shaker. Diesel leaned down to look at Mackie when she reached into the car. She winked at him to let him know that things were going fine. She almost laughed because she could see that he was pissed that the trooper was flirting.

"Here you go sir," Mackie handed him her driver's license. He covered her hand with his and held it a while.

"I'll be right back," he told her. His partner met him back at their squad car. He had Diesel's driver's license. They needed to check both of them for any warrants. This gave Diesel and Mackie a chance to talk. Diesel asked her what the trooper was saying. Mackie told him not much; just being a typical man. Diesel turned and gave him a pissed off glare.

"Diesel," Mackie scolded. "Play this cool, we are almost on our way."

The troopers walked back up. They'd acted like they were running both Diesel and Mackie's driver licenses through the database. They turned the dash camera off. They would just tell dispatch that the camera was acting up again, shutting on and off by itself.

"Well sir, it looks like we are going to have to take you in," one of them stated. "You have an outstanding warrant back in Dallas."

"What?" Diesel stated.

"He said there's a warrant for your arrest," the other trooper said.

"I think what my friend means is that he couldn't possibly have a warrant because he has never even had a parking ticket before," Mackie interrupted.

"We can do a more in-depth check when we get to the station," the trooper stated.

"Is that really necessary? My mother is dying at hospital in Houston. We were trying to get there before she takes a turn for the worst," Diesel spoke.

The trooper's looked at each other. "Well, we might be able to work something out."

"Ok, we're open to working something out," Mackie said. "I have cash, how much?" Mackie was sure she had enough money with her to satisfy whatever amount they wanted.

"That something that I'm talking about doesn't require cash," the trooper said, while looking at Mackie's breasts.

"What the hell are you talking about?" Diesel interrupted. He watched as the trooper allowed his eyes to roam all over Mackie's body.

"We are all adults here. Let's just be real about it," he spoke to Diesel. "Your girl is fine as hell. A fucking beauty queen with a banging ass body. Me, I'm checking for her lips. I want her to put her mouth on me. My partner here is an ass man. He wants to hit it from the back."

Diesel tried to jump at the trooper doing all the talking, but Mackie stepped in front of him.

CHAPTER THIRTY-ONE
BLAZE

Blaze and Aleah hopped into his car. They buckled up and Blaze raced out of the parking lot. When he got to the major freeway, he slowed down and drove the speed limit. They were running from some unknown, but he didn't want it to turn into them being chased.

Aleah's heart was beating in overtime. She had never gotten a rush like the one she just did, running from who knows what. She and Blaze kept checking the rearview and side mirrors. Aleah finally asked, "Who are we running from?"

"I'm not sure yet. Khalil texted and told me to get you out the hospital," Blaze told her.

"Why?" Aleah asked. "Why would I need to get out of the hospital? I thought someone was after you."

Before Blaze could speak again, his phone buzzed again. It was another text message from Khalil.

Khalil: *Mutherfucka claiming that Aleah shot him. Calling the police to have her arrested. Says you're covering for her to keep her from going to jail.*

Blaze: *Stay on it*

Khalil: *Word*

"Punk ass muthafucka," Blaze growled as he banged his hands on the steering wheel.

"What?" Aleah asked.

Blaze held out his phone so that she could see the message.

"What?" Aleah shrieked this time. "Why would he say that?"

"Because he's a petty, ignorant, asshole," Blaze answered. "It's his punishment to you for seeing me. Xavier probably thought that you would always be right there by his side whenever he wanted you to be. He could run around and do whatever he wanted but the minute you said 'fuck you,' he couldn't handle it," Blaze rambled. "He was at the house that night to meet up with Mackie. You didn't do anything that he wasn't already doing."

Tears began falling from Aleah's eyes. She always knew that Xavier wasn't really feeling her, but this proves that he hated her. Aleah had never been arrested before. Had never even broken a rule while in school, and here she was possibly facing an attempted murder charge. She could spend the rest of her life in prison for something that she didn't do, all because Xavier hated her.

"I can't go to jail," Aleah cried.

Once again, she felt like Xavier was controlling her life and her future.

"I'm not going to let that happen," Blaze tried to console her.

"Jury's believe eye witnesses, especially the victim. Xavier knows that," Aleah added. "He's trying to break me."

"We won't let him. Listen to me. I am not going to let him get away with this," Blaze told her.

Blaze's phone rang. This time Khalil was calling.

"What's up?" Blaze answered.

Khalil was filling Blaze in on everything that was happening at the hospital.

"What did he say?" Aleah asked when he disconnected the phone.

"Xavier told the police that you shot him," Blaze informed. "They'll be issuing a warrant for your arrest some time tonight. The police locked down the hospital a little while ago. They are searching room to room looking for us."

"Oh my God," Aleah exclaimed as she rocked back and forth.

"This is what where going to do. I am going to take you back to the house in Frost Farms. Nobody knows about that place. I want you to stay there until you hear from either me or Khalil. Don't answer your phone if anybody calls, and don't call anybody," Blaze instructed.

"What are you going to do?" Aleah asked.

"I am going to go to the police station and confess to shooting Xavier," Blaze explained.

"But he already told them that you were just covering for me," Aleah stated.

"He did. But I'm going to tell them that he is jealous and bitter and simply trying to punish you for having an affair. It will be my word against his. They'll have to decide who they want to believe and I'll have you to collaborate my story," Blaze said. "But he doesn't have any body to back him up. My attorney is the best at what he does. He will make Xavier look like he's throwing a fucking tantrum and wasting everyone's time."

"Well I should just go with you right now. I can tell them how it really was self-defense," Aleah added. "If Xavier hadn't been shot, he would have killed us. That's exactly what I told the detective and Keya."

"It may take some time for me to get them to believe what we are saying, and I don't want you sitting in jail until they figure things out," Blaze rationalized.

Aleah thought for a moment. "Maybe we should just go ahead and move to Cayman," Aleah decided. "Both of us would be safe then. I don't have anything tying me to Dallas. My family lives in Detroit. I hardly ever see them anyway. Keya was all that I had left and right now, she probably believes everything that Xavier is saying about me."

"It would have been easier had they not been issuing a warrant for your arrest. If we try to leave the country or cross the border now, they might be waiting on us."

"Blaze, I don't want to go to jail, but I don't want you to go jail either.

"I won't. Well, maybe for just a little while. Before I was out on bail, but then I was pleading not guilty. Now that I'm going to plead guilty, we can go straight to sentencing. My attorney will push for something like probation or time served," Blaze told her.

"But that's no guarantee," Aleah told him. "What if they sentence you to life in prison?"

Blaze hadn't thought about that. He didn't see any other way out. "Aleah, I love you and I love my sister, and if that's what it takes to keep both of you safe then I am willing to do that."

Aleah's tears started again. Just when she found her Mr. Right, he could possibly be taken away from her. Not only were tears burning her eyes, they were also being scorched by hatred.

"I hate Xavier and I want him to burn in hell," Aleah uttered.

CHAPTER THIRTY-TWO
KEYA

Keya sat listening to Xavier, wondering if the medication had him mixing up his memory and how things had happened. It was hard for her to believe that Aleah would have shot him. Xavier had been beating the shit out of her for years, so why would she choose to shoot him now? It just didn't make sense to her. But he was adamant that Aleah was the one who did this and not Blaze. *Did I judge Aleah wrong?*

When Keya looked at Khalil, he had a pissed off look on his face. She could tell that he didn't believe a word that Xavier was saying. But Keya wasn't sure if that was because Blaze was his friend or not. But then again, he should be happy that Blaze would be off the hook for attempted murder. *So why wasn't he*, she thought.

"Xavier, Aleah doesn't own a gun." It was the only thing that she could think of to say.

"Are you saying that you don't believe me?" Xavier was trying to make her feel guilty.

"No, I am just wondering if you are remembering things the way that they happened. You're just waking up from a coma and you're under a lot of medications," Keya explained.

"Dammit Keya, I know who shot me," Xavier yelled.

Khalil sighed heavily.

"And what's your fucking problem? Why are you even here? Get the fuck out of my room," Xavier demanded.

"Xavier, please calm down," Keya encouraged.

They all looked towards the door as it opened.

Two Dallas Police officers walked into the room, along with the detective that had been assigned to the case.

"Good evening Mr. Thomas, we understand that you would like to make a statement regarding the identity of the person who shot you?"

"Hell yes," Xavier exclaimed.

The detective took out his pad and pencil. He was prepared to finally get to the bottom of Blaze and Aleah's lie.

"Who shot you?" the detective asked.

"My wife, Aleah Thomas."

The detective just looked at Xavier. He didn't say a word.

"Did you hear me?" Xavier asked. "I said my wife shot me."

"Are you sure Mr. Thomas?"

"Why the hell does everybody keep asking me am I sure? YES," Xavier said.

The detective made it look like he was writing Aleah's name down in his pad. But he really wrote the word LIAR! He had already sent the cup that Aleah had been drinking from the night he interviewed her for gun powder residue testing. It had only been an hour since the shooting occurred when it was tested. If Aleah had shot him, there definitely would have been gun powder residue somewhere on it. Blaze didn't have any traces of gun powder on his hands either. That meant that somebody was missing from the party. The detective had thought that Xavier was about to fill in the missing party guest.

"So when are you going to arrest her?" Xavier asked.

The detective was slow to answer but eventually said, "We'll have an arrest warrant issued for your wife and once we locate her, we will bring her into the station."

"You don't have to locate her. She's across the hall in the waiting room," Xavier informed.

The detective sent the officers across the hall to check to see if Aleah was in the waiting room. The detective was getting impatient with all the lies being told. *Maybe now that her husband was implicating her in his shooting, Aleah would be more open to telling him what really happened that night,* he thought.

The officers came back through the door stating that no one was in the waiting room. It was empty.

"She's trying to escape," Xavier yelled.

Khalil, laughed out.

The detective turned around, noticing Khalil for the first time. "Mr. Hamilton, I didn't know that you knew the victim."

"I don't. I know his sister," Khalil offered.

"My, my, my, how these lives are intertwined," the detective stated.

"Excuse me, but are you going to try to find Aleah or not?" Xavier was being a true asshole. The detective gave the officers instructions to lockdown the hospital.

"Get security to help and do a room to room search. Make it fast," he added.

Keya had stopped talking a while ago. She knew Xavier better than anybody, and she knew that he was lying. She just didn't know why. *Did he hate Aleah that much that he would allow Blaze to get away with shooting him?*

Xavier continued telling his version of what happened that night. When he finished the detective stated, "That's almost the same story that Blaze and Aleah told. Only difference is that no one can agree on who the shooter was."

The officers came back in and told the detective that Aleah was no longer in the hospital.

"There is no way that you checked all of the rooms that fast," Xavier told them.

"No sir, we didn't," one of the officers replied. "We went to the security booth and looked at the cameras. We saw Mrs. Thomas and the gentleman that she was with, run from the stairwell and out of the front door about thirty minutes ago."

"That's just great! You let her get away," Xavier stated.

"Mr. Thomas, I'm sure we can find your wife. It's not like she's a criminal and running from the police," the detective told him.

"How would they know to run?" Xavier asked.

The detective turned to look at Khalil. "I'm sure Mr. Hamilton can answer that for us. Your sister's friend here is Blaze Carter's right-hand man."

"Man, get the fuck out of here," Xavier yelled.

Khalil smirked. He leaned down and kissed Keya on the cheek. He did it more to fuck with Xavier than anything. "I'll call you later," he told her.

"The hell you will. You better lose her damn number," Xavier ordered.

When Khalil left the room, Xavier started in on Keya. "What the fuck Keya? Are you hanging out with drug dealers now?"

Keya fired right back at him. "If you can hang out with Mackie, then I damn sure can hang out with Khalil." Keya stormed out of the room.

CHAPTER THIRTY-THREE
MACKIE

When Diesel jumped at the trooper, both of them put their hands on their guns, which rested in their holsters. If Mackie hadn't stepped in front of him, there was no doubt in her mind that they would have shot him.

Mackie put her hand behind her back. She needed to signal to Diesel to play it cool. She put up two fingers as she had done many times before when they were in a tight situation. She needed him to trust her. They were out on a dark highway late at night with nobody around for miles. Not one single car had passed by them since they had been out here talking with the troopers. They had missed their last check in with Blaze. If they came up missing, nobody would even know where to start looking.

Mackie knew that she and Diesel could take these two clowns down without lifting two fingers. She and Diesel were two of Dallas' most ruthless killers. But not with them having guns that they could use at a moment's notice. Mackie continued to move her fingers up and down behind her back until she heard Diesel's breathing began to slow down. Now they were in sync.

Mackie pulled her shirt over her head. She had on a cinnamon colored bra. She stepped out her jeans displaying her matching boy cut panties. Diesel kept his eyes glued to the biggest trooper. Mackie kept her eyes glued to the one that she'd talked to on the side of the SUV. Both the troopers smiled like school boys, at the sight of Mackie's body.

She watched as their dicks grew hard with a small bulge. *They're so fucking easy*, Mackie thought. *Time to go in for the kill.*

Mackie unclasped her bra and let her girls bounce freely. She was using the big guns to take these two fools out.

"Fuck that, I want to suck the shit out of them big ass titties," the biggest trooper stated.

Diesel is going to have a field day fucking you up, Mackie thought. Mackie walked slowly towards her mark. She put a little extra bounce in her step to make her tits jiggle. The trooper in front of her grabbed his dick. *That's it, take your hand away from the gun.* The big trooper kept looking back and forth between Mackie and Diesel.

Mackie reached up and put her arms around the trooper's shoulders. She pulled his lips to hers and kissed him. Before he knew what had happened, Mackie had used all the force that she could muster to send her knee into his balls. He yelped like a dog being tortured with a knife.

The sound of the trooper's scream caused his partner to take his eyes off a Diesel for a split second. It was just enough time for Diesel to swipe him off of his feet and take his gun away. Mackie took the other officer's gun. Diesel kicked the big trooper in the face. Blood splattered in every direction. Both of the troopers lay on the ground, rolling around, moaning from the pain they'd been inflicted with.

"Talk that shit now bitch," Diesel said.

Mackie quickly grabbed her bra and shirt and put them back on.

"Get up," Mackie told them. They stumbled as best they could to their feet. "Take off all your clothes."

When they didn't budge, Mackie pointed the gun at the trooper's head. They both started taking their clothes off. Mackie picked up their cuffs and told them to walk back to their car. "Big man get in the back seat and lay face down. He did as instructed. Diesel continued to hold the gun on him. Mackie took one set of cuffs and placed one on his wrist, and the other she secured to the hook in the seat. Then she told the other troop to lay face down on top of him. He looked at Mackie like she was crazy.

"What?" Mackie said. "Your horny ass wanted to fuck me from the back, right? Lay your punk ass down and let him feel all that dick."

When he still didn't move, Mackie walked up to him and put the gun right between his eyes. "I will blow your goddam brains out and not think two fucks about it," Mackie growled.

The trooper climbed in the back and laid on top of his partner. Mackie secured him with the cuffs the same way she did the other one.

Mackie didn't know when they would be discovered, but she knew they needed to put distance between them. Any cars passing by wouldn't be able to see the troopers from the way they were sprawled out in the backseat. It was going to take for someone to walk up to the car, for them to be discovered.

"Let's go," Mackie said to Diesel.

They took off at a normal speed. They needed to move quickly but had to be smart about it.

"Are you ok?" Diesel asked.

"Yeah, I'm good." Mackie continued to look behind them, making sure they were in the clear. "What about you?" Mackie asked.

Diesel didn't answer. It did something to him to have to see Mackie use her body that way. He'd wanted to kill both the troopers, but Mackie said no. She was being smart about it. If they did get caught, she didn't want them facing a capital murder charge. They'd both get the death penalty for sure.

Mackie grabbed Diesel's hand. "I'm fine Diesel." He had that same look in his eyes that Blaze would get when somebody was messing with her. She was happy to have two men by her side who loved her to the moon and back.

Mackie pulled out her phone. She needed to check in with Blaze. If she knew her brother, he would be pacing the floor by now. They were almost forty minutes off their scheduled check-in time.

"What the hell is going on?" Blaze answered the phone.

"We ran into a problem with two troopers down around Sugarland. But we are back on the road now. We have about another hour before we reach the border," Mackie explained.

"Ok, be smart," Blaze told her. "I love you."

"I love you too," Mackie repeated.

"Tell Diesel I said thanks. Y'all have fun in Cayman."

They disconnected the call. Mackie got a bad feeling. Something wasn't right with Blaze. She knew that if she asked, he wouldn't tell her anyway. She would have to check in with Khalil once they made it to Cayman.

CHAPTER THIRTY-FOUR
BLAZE

Blaze and Aleah made it to the Frost Farms house, twenty-five minutes after leaving the hospital. Blaze was in mid-thought when his phone rang. It was Mackie. Mackie gave him a few details about what was going on with her and Diesel.

Blaze felt a little better knowing that Mackie and Diesel were so close to the border. Now he could focus on trying to clear him and Aleah. Blaze wondered what Mackie had done to the state troopers. If he knew his sister and he did, it was something huge and fucked up. It was the only way she knew how to do things. He would definitely need to watch CNN tomorrow morning to find out what happened.

"I need to get down to the police station," Blaze stated.

"Please don't go," Aleah begged. "I need you."

"I need you too, Leah," Blaze stated. "But you know what I have to do."

"At least stay the night with me. You can go down to the station in the morning, please," Aleah whined.

Blaze looked as though he were weighing his options. Aleah reached for his hand and placed it over her crotch. "We don't know if or how long you might be locked up. So let me take this time to make love to you like a real woman loves a real man." Aleah had repeated the same words to him that he had told her.

Blaze rubbed his hand back and forth between Aleah's legs. Blaze could feel the heat rising from her body. He gripped her crotch tightly and pulled her close to him. When he covered his lips with hers, he squeezed tighter. Aleah loved it. Blaze felt like a caveman claiming his prize. He had shown her soft and sweet. Now he wanted to take her to a new level, rough and hard.

He gripped Aleah's waist and lifted her off the floor. He forced her body against the wall, wildly kissing her as if he would never get the chance to do it again. Aleah's breathing was jagged.

"I want you so bad," Blaze spoke. He used his body to hold her against the wall, while taking his hands and ripping her shirt off. Blaze couldn't wait for her bra to be removed. He opened his mouth as wide as he could, covering as much of her breasts that would fit into his mouth. He used both hands to squeeze, tease and please her nipples. Aleah had lost control. She loved that he wanted her so badly. Enough was enough; she wanted to feel his lips, his tongue on her skin.

She reached down and unclasped her bra, giving him free reign to devour her breasts the best way that he saw fit. Blaze quickly took her nipple into his mouth. He sucked harder than he ever had before. When he heard Aleah screaming "Oh my God, oh my God, don't stop," he applied more pressure. Aleah's hands clutched the back of Blaze's head, as she pulled him as close as she could. She arched her back causing her breasts to stick out as far as they could. When she told Blaze that she was getting ready to climax, he slid one hand between her legs. He used his fingers to delve deep into her pussy. He pushed them in and out with precision. Within minutes, Aleah was howling like a pack of wolves defending their territory. Blaze loved the feel of her vaginal walls gripping and contracting around his fingers. When Blaze removed them from her folds, they were soaked with Aleah's juices. He took his hands to his lips to get a taste of her sweetness.

Aleah's body went limp in his arms. She had just experienced the best orgasm of her entire life. "I'm never giving you up," Aleah breathed.

"Music to my ears," Blaze replied.

He hoisted Aleah's limp body up over his shoulder, carrying her to the bedroom. He had plenty more to give. He planned to fuck Aleah until the sun came up if she would allow him to. Placing her body on the bed, he removed her pants. Blaze looked at Aleah; she was amazing. *Xavier is a damn fool*, he thought. Aleah was definitely his treasure.

Blaze removed his clothes. It was Aleah's turn to be in awe of his body. It was unbelievable. Everything about Blaze screamed sexy. Blaze reached out placing his hands on Aleah's legs. He pulled her body to the edge of the bed. He got down on his knees and buried his head between her thighs. He lifted Aleah knees to give him full access. He licked slowly from her ass to her clit and back down again.

"That feels so damn good Blaze," Aleah uttered.

Blaze continued with the slow grind of his tongue between Aleah's ass cheeks. The feeling was something that she had never felt before. He was on a mission and succeeding. He was turning her out. She wouldn't want another man for as long as she lived.

Aleah found herself getting ready to climax for a second time. This time she couldn't get any words out. She now knew what women were talking about when they said their man had them speaking in tongues. Blaze was learning her body and her body language. He knew that she was close to exploding. He moved his mouth up to her folds and took as much of her pussy in his mouth as he could. He sucked hard while at the same time, sending his tongue in and out of her hot spot. Once again, Aleah howled like a pack of wolves.

Blaze wasn't done yet. That was just the warm up. He wondered how much more Aleah could take. He planned to find out. He kept Aleah on the edge of the bed. He stood up, placing Aleah's legs on his shoulders. He clutched her ass and lifted her pussy up to meet his dick. Sliding into her felt good. Blaze threw his head back, as her pussy adjusted to the width of his penis. It was snug. Aleah could feel the muscles in his dick vibrating.

Blaze started slow. He wanted Aleah to feel every inch of him. Blaze loved watching her face as she took all of him. She had the most amazing fuck face. Most of the women that Blaze had been with looked like demons when taking the rod, but Aleah's face was angelic. Blaze began increasing his pace. He was in full swing. By the sounds that Aleah was making, he knew she was on her way to third orgasm of the night. Blaze was on his was to ecstasy right along with her. In the middle of both Aleah and Blaze cumming at the same time, they heard what sounded like a mini explosion. Locked together experiencing an ultimate high, they couldn't move. FBI and DEA swarmed the room.

"Freeze," Agent Blanton yelled.

Blaze dropped his head to Aleah's chest. She rubbed the back of his head in a soothing motion. He raised his head and looked into her eyes. Tears were beginning to form.

"I love you Aleah," Blaze spoke.

"I love you Blaze," Aleah replied.

He kissed her just before Agent Blanton grabbed his arm, pulling him up off of Aleah. Aleah pulled a blanket over her to cover her body.

Blaze stood looking at her. He looked defeated. Her heart broke into a thousand pieces as she watched him being escorted from the room.

Text ROYALTY to 42828 to keep up
with our new releases!

Looking for a publishing home?

Royalty Publishing House, Where the Royals reside, is accepting submissions for writers in the urban fiction genre. If you're interested, submit the first 3-4 chapters with your synopsis to submissions@royaltypublishinghouse.com. Check out our website for more information: www.royaltypublishinghouse.com.

Be sure to <u>LIKE</u> our Royalty Publishing House
page on Facebook

CPSIA information can be obtained
at www.ICGtesting.com
Printed in the USA
BVHW041656130121
597762BV00009B/73

9 781522 864592